I0747490

Daphne Winters Psychic Investigation Series
#2

Finding Maddy

A Novel

By Deirdre Hutchins

San Joaquin Valley Press
Fresno, California

Finding Maddy is published by
San Joaquin Valley Press
P.O. Box 9485
Fresno, CA 93792
www.sanjoaquinvalleypress.com

This is a work of fiction. The characters are not based on any actual persons, living or dead. Any apparent identification with any actual person is purely coincidental.

Cover design by Andria Davis Kaye
The cover is a collage of elements from Shutterstock: Little girl says no by VIDI Studio; Curvy road, Southern California by L.A. Nature Graphics

ISBN 978-1-7378061-7-2

PROLOGUE

Madison "Maddy" Laurens had been missing for twenty years when her case hit Detective Winston Cayman's desk. Maddy's parents had reported her missing when she didn't make it home from school one fateful day.

Only her bike and blood were ever found.

They had the crime scene—an abandoned house at the end of the street where the Laurens family home was. It was covered in Maddy's blood, her hair samples found on the scene, her bike found out front.

Detective Cayman stared at the practically empty file on his desk. He was used to getting the tough ones. The files with nothing to go on. No DNA evidence of the murderer. No witnesses. If there had been anything, the Homicide Detectives would have solved it decades ago.

But this was his specialty. Cold cases no one else wanted. Or had time for.

And his record was astounding.

He was opening and closing cold cases for the Los Angeles Police Department at an exceptional rate. Sure, he was a great cop. His instincts were on point and he worked every lead until he was blurry-eyed from sleep deprivation. But it wasn't only his skills that improved his record. Detective Cayman had a secret weapon.

When case files were exceptionally thin, he pulled in a psychic named Daphne Winters.

She was quirky and snarky, characteristics he didn't normally love in a woman. But he couldn't deny that she was good at her job.

It had taken all of about fifteen minutes to realize he was going to need Daphne for the Maddy Laurens case. There simply wasn't enough in the case files to know where to begin. Unfortunately, this case stumped even Daphne.

All he ever got out of her was a nondescript sketch

and something about the mountains. Was Maddy buried there? Was the man who killed her hiding out there? What was the connection to the mountains? They never knew for sure.

And there were a lot of mountains in Southern California.

They had gone on a few wild goose chases and gotten nowhere.

Detective Cayman sighed, leaning back in his chair. Eventually, there were other cases and he couldn't spend his days on a case with no end in sight when other cold cases needed his time and energy.

He lifted the thin case file for Maddy Laurens and placed it on a stack near his filing cabinet. He wasn't putting it away, just setting it aside. He knew in his heart that one day, somehow, something would pop up that would break this case wide open.

And he'd be ready when it did.

1.

"Are you sure you want to just vigilante-justice this case?" Miguel asked Daphne as she stood in the California sun, staring at the mountain that had for so many years haunted her dreams. "We could go to the authorities."

Daphne didn't respond for a moment. It wasn't that she wanted to ignore Miguel, like she did so many other people. It was more that she just didn't have the words. Emotions often washed over her in waves. As a psychic, she found it difficult sometimes to know whose emotions she was even feeling. Was it her own obsession with finding Maddy that was making her want to punch something right now?

"We can go to the authorities when there is a reason to," Daphne blurted in her usual blunt way. Then, to get him to stop talking, she said, "Now let me work."

Daphne opened her mind to the feelings and senses all around her as she took the first step on the walking trail in front of her. It was as familiar to her as an old family heirloom. She had walked this path countless times—both with her own two feet and in the many dreams she had had about this case. The truth was here. She just knew it.

Miguel followed her silently. And she thanked him in her mind for his compliance. Yes, he had seen her work before on their case in Fresno, but this one was different. This was "the" case. The case she never solved. The case that haunted her to this day.

Fortunately, Miguel understood.

As a homicide detective, he knew all too well about the cases that plagued you. And he was here willingly supporting Daphne as she tried to silence the ghost of Maddy Laurens.

Miguel had taken a bullet to the shoulder just a week prior and his arm was still bandaged and in a sling, although it was feeling much better. He still didn't bounce up the hill with gusto. He was too afraid he might trip on a rock or something and reopen his wound.

But he wasn't going to let Daphne go onto a random trail in the Santa Monica Mountains without him. There could be thieves, thugs, perverts.

Of course, he knew well that Daphne could handle herself. She had taken down two goons—and saved his life—with the help of a ghost. But still. His protective instincts were just too strong. He watched her bound up the trail, as he followed slowly, his eye on her the whole time.

"Can you at least give me a clue what we're looking for?" Miguel called up the mountain.

She stopped long enough to turn around and roll her eyes, but then continued forward. *He* was the detective. He should detect. While she continued using senses others rarely tapped into.

And, also, she wasn't really sure what they were looking for.

Something. Anything that would propel the case

forward. She just suspected she would know it when it came to her. That's how it always was on cases: She opened her mind and it just came to her.

Daphne continued climbing the same trail. Past the same rocks and shrubs, the same expansive views of the valley before her. There was a tree on her left and she left the well-worn path to go over to it. A flash of something popped into her mind but then left it just as quickly. She looked around.

Nothing.

There was supposed to be something. But nothing was coming to her. How many times had Maddy led her up this path? The answers *had* to be here.

"Shit, shit, shit." Daphne punched the tree, her frustration overwhelming her. Why did this case elude her?

She had worked on so many cases in the past. And most of the time, the truths and revelations came to her without even trying. The ghosts would tell her what she needed to know. Or an image would flash in her mind that would give them some sort of direction. But with Maddy Laurens...there was nothing. An emptiness. A black hole where insight and information should be.

Miguel finally caught up to her and thankfully remained silent as he squinted into the sun. The view of the city was beautiful from up here, and he tried to focus on that rather than the fact they were up here in the first place. Some part of Maddy's story took place on this mountain and he knew the reality of that.

But he was off the clock, so he didn't want to think about it.

Daphne circled the tree, her hands extended in front of her. Her gut told her this tree had meaning, but her senses were picking up nothing. After a complete rotation, she kicked the tree. "Shit!"

A couple hiking up the trail they had been on moments ago looked over at Miguel and Daphne and stared. I am sure a man in a sling and a woman kicking a tree were a bit of a curiosity.

Miguel just smiled and waved in a way that said,

"Nothing to see here." But Daphne, if she even noticed the couple, completely ignored them and their staring. What did their trivial judgments matter in a universe as big as this one, anyway? They knew nothing of what Maddy had suffered. They would go home to their perfect Los Angelino life, drive a fancy sports car and look down on peasants. But they were the ones Daphne felt sorry for.

Because they were completely ignorant to real life.

"I don't get it." Daphne ran a hand through her spiky blonde hair and leaned against the tree as she sat in the dirt. "Why is nothing coming through?"

Miguel didn't have the first clue how to answer her question, so he countered with one of his own. "Has this ever happened to you before?"

Daphne shook her head. "Never."

Miguel sat in the dirt next to Daphne. Normally, he wouldn't want to get himself dirty, but right now it felt more important to be there for her. "And you've been to this trail before, right?"

Daphne looked straight into his eyes in her way of looking right through you. "Many times."

"Don't take this the wrong way, but maybe you need to try something different." Miguel braced himself for an angry outburst from Daphne, but it didn't come. She sighed instead.

Daphne leaned her head back against the tree. "It's hard to explain, but I just know the answers are here."

Miguel leaned forward and gently grasped Daphne's hand. "I believe you. And it's probably true. But what if this is step two?"

Daphne raised an eyebrow at Miguel.

Miguel continued. "Maybe you aren't meant to start here. Maybe this is where it ends." Miguel stood and pulled Daphne up with him. "I don't mean to brag, but I know a thing or two about investigating homicides without ghosts."

Daphne snorted in response.

"Why don't you start at the beginning and tell me everything you know?" Miguel added.

Daphne stared at the tree one last time. There was something there. But how many times would she come here and get nowhere? It couldn't hurt to try it the old-fashioned way. With a sidelong glance at the tree, Daphne started back to the trail, Miguel holding her hand with his one good one.

"Well, there isn't much to go on," she said. "They only ever found her bike and her murder scene. It was covered in her blood but not much else. There was no forensic evidence of the perp at all."

"Where did it take place?"

"An abandoned house on the corner near where Maddy lived. It seemed like she never made it home from school that day."

"But she went to school that day?"

Daphne nodded. "Yes, the teacher confirmed that she was in class all day."

"Have you been to the abandoned house?"

"Many times. It's since been demolished and rebuilt and a family lives there now. They probably don't even know the sinister things that took place there all those years ago."

"And Maddy's ghost didn't give you a bunch of clues?"

"Well, first of all, she was eight. But also, she visits me in dreams. I don't see her physically like I did Grace Collins." Grace was the ghost on their last case in Fresno.

"What did she describe?"

"Tall, skinny, bald, Caucasian. Nothing helpful except..."

"Except what?"

"Well, he had a tattoo on his arm. She got a good look at it too."

"Oh, that's great. It's a start anyway."

"It's not, actually. Because whenever she would try to show it to me, it would disappear from my mind. This case is really frustrating because I can't grasp any details. They're always just out of reach."

Miguel looked out at the view again. The sun was high in the sky and it was getting hot. There was very little shade out here and the sun was intense. Luckily the heat didn't really bother him, but he knew they would need to replenish with water soon. "Huh. I wonder why."

Daphne shrugged. She had never understood why this case was so elusive. Normally things popped in her head whether she liked it or not, but with this case she couldn't get any details try as she might. "It's just one of those things, I guess."

"And you're sure it's never happened before?" Miguel stopped walking and squinted as he looked at Daphne, the sun bright in his eyes.

Daphne shook her head vehemently. "That's what drives me crazy about this case."

"Then it's not just one of those things. It's something specific to *this* case. It's hiding your abilities somehow."

Daphne huffed. "That's not a thing."

"What if the murderer's dead and his ghost is getting in the way and sending mixed signals or something?"

"Not possible. I'd be able to sense him. The murderer is alive."

"Then we can find him. Maybe Maddy can describe the tattoo to you instead of showing you. Would that work?"

Daphne shook her head. "Maddy never talks. On the rare occasions when her ghost visits me, she just stares at me. Except in my dreams. In my dreams, she begs me to find her and always leads me here. To this trail. Where everything goes cold."

Miguel shook his head. "I don't know, Daph. Something is different with this case. I know I am new to your methods, but you had clear and vivid details with Grace's ghost and your prior record is untarnished on every case. Why this case?"

"I don't know. But it looks like this time we're going to have to investigate without psychic abilities. Where do we start, Detective?"

"Where we always start. The crime scene."

"Then we'll need the case file. Come on. I'll take

you to the crime scene photos."

2.

Detective Winston Cayman had a love-hate relationship with retirement.

He loved the freedom to do the things he'd always dreamed about. He got a lot more fishing in than when he was younger. Spent a lot more time at home, too. But he missed solving cases and providing closure to families. And the part he missed most of all was catching the people who thought they'd committed the perfect crime. Like he was some sort of avenging angel.

It may take ten, twenty, even fifty years, but it always caught up to them. Never do anything in the shadows you don't want seen in the light.

As he continued working on his crossword puzzle in the living room, the sunlight streaming across his face, he felt a lack of purpose in this freedom. And it bothered him.

His wife, Helen, had quit her career right after they'd had kids since his schedule was so erratic. Her life's purpose had been caring for the family and raising the kids. And she'd done a helluva job at it, too. Their kids were stellar human beings and he could take very little credit for it.

And he'd debated talking his son out of following in his footsteps to become a cop. But of course his son had chosen this career path. Winston's obsession with his cases made it seem glamorous. Helen had often accused him of being married to the force. But it wasn't the force. It was closing cases that Winston was in love with.

Derek hadn't made Detective yet, but he would soon. It was only a matter of time. Winston had been a well-respected member of the law enforcement community and Derek would reap the benefits of that. He walked in from the Academy more popular than the other cadets simply because of Winston's record.

And, logically, Winston knew it was time to pass

the baton to the younger generation. He'd always been a big guy, and now on his older bones, the physical weight wore him out much more quickly.

But his mind was still sharp.

So he daydreamed from time to time of closing just one more case. Of digging through the clues no one else could see and connecting dots that were barely on the page. Of solving that case that everyone thought was unsolvable.

Winston sighed, noting that his mind had completely wandered from the puzzle at hand. He stared out the window, seeing the past in his mind's eye. But as he stared, he saw a small nondescript sedan slow down and then park.

Right in front of his house.

Years on the force heightened his alarm bells to things that were out of the ordinary. What was this car doing here? He walked briskly over to the window and hid his body behind the curtain so he could watch the driver of the strange car without their knowledge that they were being scoped.

He saw the car door slowly open and a Mexican man climb out. Winston noticed he was dressed professionally, hair slicked back and nicely styled, yet he had his left arm in a sling. Nothing made sense yet, so he continued spying as a woman with spiky blonde hair climbed out of the passenger seat.

And then he breathed a sigh of relief.

He knew that hair and that bohemian style of clothing anywhere. Daphne. But he still had no idea why he was seeing this odd couple in his front yard.

Detective Cayman opened the front door and tightened his lips into a hard line. He looked like a scolding parent, his arms folded across his broad chest.

From halfway up the walkway, Daphne stated to the old man, "Retirement did nothing for your mood, I see."

"Why are you at my house?" He stuck his chin out as he spoke.

As she approached him, Daphne grabbed

Detective Cayman's hand from where it was tucked in his arm and gave it a warm squeeze. "It's good to see you, too, Detective."

And then the old guy broke, a smile creeping across his face. He should've known better than to try and intimidate a woman who was more in touch with your thoughts and feelings than you were. He grabbed her into a bear hug and held her tight. The hug was warm, but over her shoulder he eyeballed Miguel.

Sensing his distrust of the stranger, Daphne explained unprompted, "This is Detective Miguel Alvarez. Fresno P.D. homicide."

At the name, Winston's face softened. He remembered talking to Detective Alvarez on the phone about Daphne.

"So you learned that she's the real deal, huh?" Winston asked.

Miguel snuck a sideways glance at Daphne and smiled. "Something like that."

"We're not here for a social visit, Winston."

Daphne got straight to the point. "We're here about Maddy Laurens."

"What prompted the cobwebs to be dusted off that old case?" Winston asked. His face was stern, but Daphne could see the twinkle in his eye.

"I still dream about her. All the time. I have to at least find her body so her family can have some closure."

"Ah. Chasing the one that got away, I see." Detective Cayman turned around, leaving the door wide open behind himself, passive-aggressively telling Miguel and Daphne to follow.

Daphne marched right in, but Miguel hesitated for a moment. He didn't know this guy at all and he definitely wasn't getting the feeling that Detective Cayman was eager to work in his retirement. Daphne, of course, knew better. She knew Winston was just a gruff exterior.

Winston turned right into a kitchen that faced the front yard. There were barstools at an island and he offered his visitors a seat by way of a gesture with his hand. "Is it the only case you never solved?"

Daphne nodded as she and Miguel sat down.

"Yeah, me too," Winston responded. "Those ones always haunt your dreams. Hell, I'm not even psychic and I still hear Maddy calling for me."

Daphne stuck a thumb in Miguel's face. "This guy is on medical leave while his shoulder heals, so we decided to see if we could make any headway on Maddy Laurens in the meantime."

Winston nodded toward Miguel. "Took one for the team, huh, Detective?"

Miguel rubbed his sore shoulder instinctually. "Yeah. I was shot on the last case where a ghost was calling all the shots."

Detective Cayman tossed his head back and laughed, a deep barrel-chested hearty laugh. "I told you her methods were effective. I never said they weren't completely wild and unpredictable."

Daphne didn't come here to fill Cayman in on the Grace Collins case, so she jumped right in to what she did want to talk about. "We need the crime scene photos."

Detective Cayman didn't answer right away. He walked over to the cabinet and grabbed a glass, filling it with water from the fridge. "I was fishing at Bass Lake not too long ago. I've started fishing a lot more in my retirement. There was a really large trout that had been circling my boat. I'd had a great day on the water, catching tons of things, including a milk carton, by the way. But that trout just kept circling. I tried chasing him, forcing him, coercing him. He wasn't biting. As a last-ditch effort I leaned over the boat and tried to grab him with my own two hands."

Daphne sneered at her old partner. "Don't distract me. I need those photos."

Winston ignored her and continued. "You know what happened? I fell in. Had water and muck in every crack and crevice. Lost my favorite hat, too." He leaned forward and wagged a finger in her face. "If you chase elusive fish, you're going to fall in."

Daphne rolled her eyes and then shoved his wagging finger. "Who do you think you're fooling? You want to solve this case as much as I do. And you know why you fell in? Because you had nothing better to do than chase a stupid fish. So you can either help me find Maddy or you can hand me her case file and get back to staring out your window. But either way, I'm doing this."

"I thought I heard voices." A beautiful woman in her sixties waltzed into the kitchen.

Winston stood up straight, a stern look plastered across his face again. "This is my wife, Helen. Helen, these are some old colleagues wanting to open up a cold case."

Helen looked at the group in her kitchen and then smirked. Daphne could sense she was no fool. She knew her husband was only really happy when he was on the hunt.

"Well, doesn't that sound like a fun activity?" Helen said, reaching across her husband and grabbing an apple from the fruit bowl.

"I'm retired," Winston growled to no one in particular.

"I know, honey." Helen patted his arm and then

waltzed back out of the kitchen.

Daphne and Winston stared at each other for a moment. A couple of stubborn souls, Miguel noticed. But he was only here to help Daphne, and if Detective Cayman wasn't eager to help in his retirement, Miguel could respect that. He stood up from the barstool. "It's okay if you don't want to get involved, Detective Cayman. We understand. But can you share with us what you have? Daphne can't move on until she gets somewhere with this case."

Winston's eyes stayed locked on Daphne as she responded, "He's going to help us. He just wants to play out the part where he pretends retirement is better than solving cold cases. But he's just about to realize everyone knows it's B.S."

Winston leaned across the bar one more time, his face inches from Daphne's. "Well, that's where you're wrong, little miss psychic. I already knew everyone could see right through me."

Daphne rolled her eyes. "Okay, I meant 'admit',

not 'realize. But either way, I know you need the closure as much as I do."

"Slightly wrong again. I do appreciate the closure, but I need something too do besides fishing and crossword puzzles."

"Just get the file, Cayman," Daphne instructed. She remained seated in her barstool, never wavering in the knowledge that Detective Cayman was part of the team with her and Miguel.

Miguel, less convinced, stood there watching the scene play out.

The staring contest between Daphne and Cayman continued for another minute, before he broke off and left the room heading toward a short hallway off the kitchen. When he returned, he had a very thin manila folder in his hand.

Slapping it on the counter he announced, "I know why you want to see these, Alvarez, but it won't help."

Miguel didn't see a reason to argue since he was new to the case, so he responded, "I always start with the crime scene."

Cayman folded his arms, not offering to open the folder for his visitors. "Homicide is different. You're hot on a warm trail. Like a dog on the hunt. Cold cases are more like finding pieces to a mosaic strewn all over the lawn and you have to put them back together into a beautiful, cohesive picture."

Daphne grabbed the folder and opened it, pulling out two grisly photographs.

"This is the house," Daphne said, handing the first photograph to Miguel. It contained a typical ranch style home like you would expect to see in the San Fernando Valley, with a pink bike on its side in the driveway. It was a little unkempt, but otherwise a lovely-looking home to raise a family in. Not that murder was ever acceptable, but the five-o-clock news didn't care about most of them. This was the type of neighborhood that would cause a scandal that the media wouldn't be able to resist. Beautiful Caucasian girl in a middle-class suburban home…. The kind of bullshit they ate right up like candy.

"And this is what was inside." Daphne handed the second photograph to Miguel robotically, like it was no big deal. She'd seen it a thousand times and it only served to frustrate her that she couldn't sense anything from this case. But Miguel's eyes widened at what he saw.

It was one of the most gruesome crime scenes he'd ever seen. And he'd seen his share.

In his line of work, he mostly saw gunshot wounds. A jilted lover getting revenge. A drug deal gone south. Those deaths weren't exactly tidy, but they were contained.

What he saw before him was most definitely not contained.

It was a small living room, he assumed, because he saw a sliding glass door in the background and a fireplace in the corner. There was no furniture. But none of that was as jarring as the blood splatter. It was everywhere. On the walls. On the floor. A bit on the ceiling. He expected to see writing on the wall like a serial killer might do. The scent of death came back to his memory, as if he were standing in that very room.

"This looks like more than one person's blood. How can a little girl cover this much space?"

"Looks like he didn't waste a single drop, eh?" Winston leaned across the counter, pointing at a wall in the photograph. "We never found a body so there's no C.O.D. confirmed, but Crime Scene determined that based on the blood splatter here, this was the death blow."

"Did they have a theory on murder weapon?" Miguel asked.

"Oh yeah. They thought maybe an axe. For sure, something more forceful than a switchblade."

At Cayman's words, Daphne winced. An image of a pickaxe appeared unbidden in her mind's eye and she watched it swing down toward a little girl. An awful chill came over her as she realized she heard and saw the death blow. "It wasn't an axe. It was the smaller one. A pickaxe."

Winston breathed through his nose at the words, tightening his lips. "That'd do it," he growled.

"You saw this? You finally sensed something?" Miguel put a hand on Daphne's back, knowing full well what a curse it must be to see intimate details of a child's murder. Daphne looked up at Miguel, disgust plastered across her face. She nodded. "That's good, right?"

"It's downright unbelievable," Cayman said. "This is the first clue we've gotten in twenty-seven years."

"So now we have something to go on, thanks to Daphne. Is there someone at the force we need to tell that we're reopening this case?" Miguel picked up the other pieces of paper in the file. A few statements from Maddy's parents and her teacher, a police sketch, and a crime lab report, but not much else.

"I can let the Chief know, just to be respectful," Detective Cayman answered. "But unless your last name is Laurens, the only other people in the world who care about what happened to Maddy are right here in this room."

"Okay, then let's get started. Murder weapon is a big deal. And pickaxe is uncommon," Miguel stated. He was ready to start digging in even with what little they had to start with.

"I think you guys might be missing a big point," Daphne stated. She fought off the beginnings of a headache. "Why, after all these years, did something suddenly come through? Something's changed."

3.

"Let me run in and talk to Derek," Cayman instructed. "No one would think twice about a father visiting a son, but all of us? That's bound to turn some heads."

"So he became a cop after all?" Daphne asked. She'd known Derek as a teenager and had always liked the young carbon copy of his gruff old man. He hadn't had the chance last time she saw him to fill out and become barrel-chested like Winston, but he had the height and the body type to be just as much of a bear.

"Of course, he did," was all she heard grumbled as Winston climbed out of the car.

Miguel sat in the driver's seat looking at the few papers that had been in the Maddy Laurens cold case file. "The murder scene and weapon are so unique. Of course, you guys cross-referenced to similar cases across the country?" He was asking, but also instructing.

And Daphne didn't bother answering one way or the other. She assumed Cayman had done his homework. He was a good cop. But her role had always been different. She didn't look things up in databases or read reports. She told him everything she sensed and he listened.

But with this case, nothing had ever popped into her head in years of working on it. Until now. And for some reason she couldn't put her finger on, that bothered her.

Daphne wasn't used to living in a world of uncertainty. All her life she had just *known* things. She was five when she'd just blurted out the old family secret about grandma and her secret affair. And how that man had actually fathered her aunt and uncle. Thanks to Daphne's gift, the affair hadn't been so secret after that.

And no one could do anything in the Winters household that Daphne didn't know about. Even if she couldn't sense it automatically, there was always some ghost or spirit willing to tattle. So she'd never not had a way to get to the bottom of things. It didn't do much to improve her popularity within the family, that was for sure.

"There must be a ghost involved," Daphne stated out loud.

Miguel placed the papers on his lap and smiled. "Isn't there always?"

"Shut up." Daphne slapped his chest playfully before continuing. "Something put that image in my head. And I've tried so many times before. For years. I've dreamt about this case, begged Maddy for clues. And nothing. So why now? In the past, it's always been because of a spirit."

"Can't you just ask it? The ghost that's helping you?"

"Yes, that would be amazing. But I'm not sensing any ghost." Daphne frowned. "I don't know who I'd be talking to. It's super frustrating."

Miguel frowned empathetically with Daphne. He

didn't really have any tips, since he'd never relied on ghosts to get his information. But he did know how to follow breadcrumbs. "Maybe one ghost could lead us to another? Like when I interview witnesses. I start with everyone who knew the victim and then those conversations lead me to my next round of interviews."

Daphne perked up. "Cayman had said unless your last name was Laurens, you probably didn't care about this old case anymore. Maybe one of her relatives or a parent died recently and is trying to help get the case solved from the spirit world. She did disappear 27 years ago."

"That can't be too hard to find out. We can check public records for death certificates when Detective Cayman gets back," Miguel responded.

Daphne frowned again, flopping back against the seat. "But why can't I sense them? This case is bizarre. I don't just talk to ghosts, Miguel. I *see* them. But right now? Literally nothing."

"But in the past those ghosts have wanted to be seen, right? Maybe they have different ways to communicate and this one doesn't want you to know who they are."

Daphne had a deep crease in her brow as she turned concerned eyes toward Miguel. "But why not?"

Miguel gently rested his palm against her cheek. He was a little frustrated himself, not really knowing how to help Daphne. He just sensed her worry and didn't know what else to do but comfort her. She leaned into his hand and then turned her head and quickly kissed his palm.

"I knew it. I knew something was going on with you two." Cayman opened the backseat passenger door and climbed in.

"What does that make you? Sherlock Holmes? Why would Miguel be here on his medical leave if he didn't love me?" Daphne rolled her eyes and Miguel just laughed.

"It was inevitable that you would end up with a cop," Cayman responded.

This caused Daphne to turn around in her seat to look him squarely in the eyes. "Why do you say that?"

"You come with a lot of baggage for such a small woman." Detective Cayman wagged a finger in her face. "Always blurting out uncomfortable truths. Talking about dead people. Who else was going to find those qualities attractive?"

Daphne folded her arms across her chest but said nothing. She knew she wasn't everyone's cup of tea. She'd been told that since she was a child. But knowing why a policeman would be best able to put up with her, she couldn't say.

Miguel, on the other hand, laughed out loud. "After I got done thinking she was crazy, I have to say I got a little bit obsessed with her."

"Let me guess. You realized that in her own quirky way she was just like you?" Cayman smirked.

"Are you two finished? Miguel's leave doesn't last forever and we have a little girl to find," Daphne scolded.

"Oh, yeah, about that." Cayman shifted in his seat as if he'd suddenly remembered the case that had haunted him and Daphne for years. "Get this. There was a serial killer in the 90's that killed people with a pickaxe. The M.O. isn't completely the same, but it's unique enough that I think it at least gets us going."

"That's incredible," Miguel responded. "See, Daphne? Breadcrumbs. We don't have to have all the answers day one. You got us a murder weapon, that got us a lead."

"This guy was based in Arizona, at least as far as anyone knows. And he killed young women, not little girls. But he's tied to at least six deaths and he used a pickaxe every time," Cayman explained.

"We have to talk to this guy," Miguel said.

"It'd be quite the trip. He's in a maximum-security prison in Florence Arizona," Cayman responded. "We could always get a phone interview."

"Daphne needs to be in the room with him to sense if he's telling the truth." Miguel gestured in Daphne's direction across the center console. "It can't be more than a day's drive, right?"

Cayman rubbed his hands together. "That's true.

We could take turns driving and not even need to stop."

Daphne held up her hands. "As much as I love to be the litmus test for serial killers, can we please start by finding out whose ghost is helping me? Before we drive to a maximum-security prison in Florence Arizona, we need to swing by public records and find out which Laurens family member died."

Cayman slapped his forehead. "I don't know why I didn't think of this before! I already know who it is. Maddy's father, Xavier, died about six months ago. It was all over the news like the story was fresh or something."

"Oh, that has to be it!" Miguel responded. "Who else would be as vested to find his daughter's killer?"

"You mean besides Maddy?" Daphne raised an eyebrow. Something wasn't feeling right about the whole thing, but logically she knew they were right. Xavier Laurens would be the one spirit who would want to help her more than any other. "But why is he staying hidden?"

"Is there a way to force him to show himself? Talk to you directly instead of playing all these games?" Miguel asked.

Daphne nodded. "There is. And I might need some help to do it."

"Perfect. Let's talk to Maddy's father and then maybe we won't have to drive to Arizona at all. How do we get started?" Miguel asked.

"Start the car." Daphne put on her seatbelt as she instructed Miguel in the next steps. "I'll tell you how to get to my friend Duncan's apartment." She sat up straight and looked out the window in front of her, having no idea how her next words would be taken. "We're going to have a séance."

Miguel froze at the words but said nothing. It was Cayman who groaned and said, "I knew there was going to be something extreme before we got to the end of this!"

Daphne rolled her eyes, although she had partially been expecting resistance. "It won't be the craziest thing you've done in your career, believe me. Now drive, Miguel."

4.

"What's up with Dad lately?" Officer Derek Cayman was standing in the kitchen of his childhood home talking to his mother. He had a small window on his lunch break before he had to get back to work.

Helen was making a sandwich for her son as if no time had passed and he was still a tow-headed boy in his dinosaur pajamas instead of the barrel-chested man before her standing there in his police uniform. "What do you mean, monkey?"

She had been calling him monkey since he was three and he liked to climb the dressers and furniture in the house. Again, despite the fact he was all grown up, the childhood nickname had stuck.

"He's working a cold case that he shouldn't be

working. He came by asking for information about some serial killer."

Helen shook her head as she cut the sandwich in half. "It shouldn't surprise you that your father is bored. He just needs something meaningful to do. And that psychic he used to work with showed up and got him all excited again." She handed him the sandwich she'd made and he eagerly took a bite.

No one made sandwiches like his mother.

Still chewing, he tucked the food to one side and said, "Yeah, but he should be letting the actual police work on it. He's retired."

Helen smiled with wistful eyes. As a police wife, she had grown to be a lot tougher than she looked. She'd seen a lot, supported a lot, and shielded her family from so much. More than they'd ever know. And she was proud of that. Her children had had a somewhat normal childhood despite what her husband brought home with him every day: murders, kidnappings, rapes, suicides. So much darkness.

"This is a cold case no one else was working. And you know your father wasn't going to sit idly by while someone else works what he feels is *his* case. How would you feel if you were him?"

Derek swallowed and stared at his mother. She had him there and she knew it. "Yeah, but he could get hurt. He's old."

"Did you share your feelings with him?"

"Yeah, but you know how he is. Of course he didn't listen. He's so stubborn."

Helen smiled again and squeezed her son's hand. He was so much like Winston when she'd first met him. She had fond memories of a young Winston in his uniform, so proud to be a cop. "There's a fine line between passion and crazy. That's why the word 'fan' comes from fanatic. Your father gets in a zone and then he's borderline obsessed with it." Helen sighed. "Honestly, I don't think he ever left the Maddy Laurens zone just because he retired. He's been in it this whole time."

"So I should just let him run all over California and

Arizona chasing serial killers? Come on, Mom."

"Honestly? Yes."

Derek rolled his eyes at her, so she continued.

"He has Daphne Winters and that new young detective. He's not LAPD, but at least your dad isn't off on his own."

"Not LAPD? So someone with no jurisdiction, a lunatic and an old man are off hunting a serial killer?" Derek shook his head. "This is worse than I thought."

Helen picked up her iced tea and sat down at the kitchen table. "What's the worst that can happen? He feels young again? I live with the man. He's bored. No, worse than that. He feels purposeless. It's not good."

Derek thought about it for a moment. At first, he was frustrated with his father's meddling. He'd had his day—now it was time for the young blood to fight crime. And then he was worried about his father—he genuinely was.

But when he thought about how he might feel in his father's shoes, and his mother's words that his dad felt like he had no purpose, he felt a little sympathy. He wouldn't want to be in his seventies with nothing to do all day. And a case you never solved hanging over your head constantly.

"He's miserable?" Derek asked his mother.

"I wouldn't necessarily say miserable. But I do think this case has revitalized a piece of him he never actually put to rest when he retired."

"I can probably make a few calls." Derek took another bite. "Everyone on the force still loves Dad. He's a legend. I'll bet if he wanted to work on a case now and again, all he had to do was ask."

Helen beamed. She knew Winston Cayman was well-regarded for his service. And she was really proud of him. After all the sacrifices she'd made so he could be so great at his job, she felt the tiniest pride that she had a piece in his successes. Every family that got closure thanks to Winston was in part Helen's success too.

"I'm sure he'd like that. Maybe start by seeing if the cold case of Maddy Laurens can officially be reopened?

Then he wouldn't be going rogue, but working on an actual case in some capacity." Helen made the suggestion to her son, not sure if there was even a real chance of it.

But Derek seemed to consider it as he rubbed his chin. "Okay. I'll talk to the Chief. I don't want him feeling unfulfilled."

"He'll never admit it, but I think he would like working with you too," Helen said just before she sipped her iced tea.

"He didn't even want me to become a cop." Derek looked skeptical at his mother's words. But she knew best. She knew what Winston meant even when he himself wasn't sure.

"No. He didn't want you to lose nights, weekends, soccer games and school plays to cases that consumed you. He was protecting you when he said those words. He's proud of you."

Helen's words stunned Derek for a moment, they were such a paradigm shift. His father had said so many unkind words trying to dissuade Derek from choosing his same career path. But the truth was painfully right there all along and his mother was right.

They were words of love and support, not disapproval and derision.

With only a few bites left, Derek lifted what was left of his sandwich. "Thanks for the sandwich, Mom."

And he went back to work, the job that he and his father both cared deeply about. Of that much in this world, he was certain.

5.

Miguel parked the car next to the ugliest building he'd ever seen in his life. "Are you sure your friend lives here?"

If there was an apartment manager, he was not doing his job. There were boarded up windows on every floor. Paint was barely still there—in fact, in many places the *stucco* wasn't even there anymore. Graffiti was the main decorating choice. Miguel had seen his share of sketchy apartment buildings, but this one topped them all.

Daphne climbed out of the car. "It'll make more sense when you meet him." She looked up at the clear, blue, Southern California sky. Back in Fresno it would just be suffocatingly hot, but this was more of a warmth. She wasn't sad to have left this part of her life behind, but some part of her would always find this area of the country to be her home.

"Ah the seedy side of the San Fernando Valley. Always a pleasure to come here. Thanks, Daphne." Cayman winked at her, and she ignored him.

She bypassed the intercom at the front door and marched through a front gate that had been left wide open. This made Miguel a little nervous and his protective side kicked in. "Stay close to me, Daph."

Daphne wasn't afraid. Like, at all. Rundown buildings were just that: rundown buildings. Didn't necessarily equate to danger. But she let Miguel have his manly moment. "Second floor. Apartment 210." She slipped her hand into his good hand and Cayman followed them up the stairs to the door marked 210. Well, marked with the 2 and the 0 anyway. The 1 was just a faded discoloration where the 1 used to be.

Miguel knocked on the door, his muscles tense at the prospect of what he might find. But Daphne, calm as a summer breeze, called out, "Duncan? You home?"

"Daphne!" Miguel heard the man's voice long

before the door opened and a large man who even dwarfed Detective Cayman opened the door and put a large arm around Daphne's shoulder and squeezed. The huge smile and warmth in his eyes told Miguel that this man was genuinely happy to see the quirky psychic. And Miguel understood. Daphne had shared with him many times how Duncan and his crew were just about the only family Daphne had anymore. But in his wildest imaginations, Miguel had never pictured Daphne's extended family living in a place like this. "Why didn't you tell me you were coming? I'd have at least cleaned the place up a bit."

Daphne looked over his shoulder and saw stuff everywhere. "No, you wouldn't. But that's okay, Duncan."

Without skipping a beat or denying what Daphne had said, the large man stuck a large hand in Miguel's face. "I'm Duncan Miller. Paranormal investigator."

Miguel shook it and responded in kind. "Detective Miguel Alvarez. Fresno P.D. This is Detective Winston Cayman, L.A.P.D., cold case division."

"Retired," Cayman clarified as he shook Duncan's hand.

"Yes, Daphne has told me so much about you two. How exciting to meet you both. Please come in." Duncan turned, his head almost scraping the door jamb, and hurriedly starting shoving stuff into piles in an attempt to make the apartment look less messy. It didn't work. "I'm just getting back from that case in Minnesota we were hoping you'd help on, Daphne. Thanks for the tip, by the way. It turned out it was the land that was haunted. Cursed, actually."

Daphne shrugged. "I knew it."

"So, is this visit business or pleasure?" Duncan asked.

As if she had done it many times, Daphne shoved some clothes over on the couch and plopped down, her black boots thumping back to the floor as she did. "Well, I didn't want to come to SoCal and not see you, Duncan, but this is about a case. It's about Maddy Laurens."

Miguel and Cayman walked in slowly. Miguel tried

to make his face impassive even as the smell of spoiled milk hit his nose. He could feel his clothes getting dirty just standing there in this apartment.

"Oh, great. You're working on that again. Good for you." Duncan patted her arm in a brotherly way. He was so jolly and good-natured, it was easy for Miguel to see why Daphne felt comfortable with this man. His apartment, on the other hand, was making Miguel's skin crawl.

"Miguel was willing to help me, so we came down here to see if we could make any headway and...." Daphne leaned in to Duncan. "I actually did. I had a vision of the murder weapon."

"Whoa, that's huge, Daphne!" Duncan looked around the somber room. "Do I assume you're here because it led you to something paranormal? Or were you just excited to share this news with an old friend?"

"I need your help to do a séance," Daphne said, getting straight to the point. Life was too short for pleasantries and nonsense.

Duncan huffed a laugh. "Since when? I need *you* for séances. You usually can't stop the ghosts from coming to you."

Daphne shook her head. "I can't explain it. But somehow I know a spirit is helping me, but not in the usual way. I can't sense the spirit at all, just suddenly I got the vision of the weapon."

"What if it's not helping you, then?" Duncan asked.

Miguel stood near the couch, slightly afraid to sit, with his arms folded. "How do you mean?"

Duncan sat on the scuffed coffee table in front of where Daphne was sitting. The wrinkle of his brow was enough to show his worry over the possibilities. "If we don't know who is communicating, we can't be sure of their motives."

Daphne shook her head. "No. No, it's helping me. I just don't know who, or how, or why..."

Duncan smiled a half-smile. "You know I have never doubted your instincts."

"Then séance?" Daphne asked.

"Then séance. Let me find the bag." Duncan walked down a short hall and, opening a coat closet, rummaged around.

"I've been shot at, chased, almost run down in a car once," Cayman said, rubbing his chin, "but never once has an investigation led me to a séance. Hope this works, Daphne."

"It will," Miguel assured Cayman before Daphne could respond. "I had never had a ghost so active in her own murder investigation before my last case, but Daphne made it seem…natural somehow."

Daphne rolled her eyes. "It *is* natural." But deep down, the truth she didn't want to tell herself was that even she was a bit skeptical. Never in her life—many years of interacting with the paranormal—had she ever had anything like this happen. Something was blocking her and she couldn't figure out what. She hoped the séance was the answer, but it was just a hope. A bravado she was faking. None of her usual confidence was actually there.

But she would find Maddy Laurens with or without spirits. That much she was determined to make come true.

"Found it!"

Duncan waltzed back into the living room carrying a large black duffel bag. "Normally Duane would have me keep a better system, but when he's not around, the system falls apart."

"How shocking." Miguel couldn't resist the sarcasm.

"Duane is very particular about his equipment," Daphne explained to Cayman and Miguel.

"What kind of equipment do you use in a séance?" Cayman asked, truly curious.

Duncan plopped the bag on the ground. "Well, I keep most of my investigating equipment in bags like these—not just stuff for séances. Flashlights, voice recorders, holy water, various herbs, usually a camera or two. When I'm called to a case, I never know what I may encounter or what I may need."

"Just set it up, Duncan." Daphne knelt on the floor at Duncan's feet and he followed suit. The detectives remained standing.

Duncan dug around in the bag as he spoke. "Daphne once passed out from an aggressive ghost we encountered. Did she tell you guys about that?" Duncan pulled out several tealight candles as he spoke.

Miguel looked at Daphne. She scowled when she saw concern plastered across his face. She was patient with his need to overprotect her, but not when it came to the paranormal. Never with ghosts.

Miguel responded to Duncan that he hadn't heard the story.

"We were in Arkansas investigating a bed and breakfast." Duncan pulled out a small metallic bowl and began sprinkling dried leaves he removed from a glass jar. "The owners were total skeptics. They'd only called us because their guests kept complaining. Room 202, I believe, was the one that guests kept leaving. Remember, Daphne?"

"I remember," Daphne mumbled with about a tenth of the gusto Duncan was portraying.

"Well, it turned out, room 202 wasn't anything to worry about." Duncan dug around in his bag and pulled out a lighter, slowly lighting each of the tealight candles he'd arranged in a small circle around the metal bowl. "Sure, it was some lady who had died and her spirit was still trapped there, but she was gentle and kind. People would see the rocking chair in the room rocking by itself, hear footsteps, sometimes even see her apparition, but never anything harmful." He sat up, lighter mid-air. "But. The place was haunted by an angry ghost. And it wasn't confined to room 202. You want to tell them what happened, Daphne?"

Daphne's only answer was her death stare. If she could make him stop talking with a look, Duncan would've frozen right then and there.

But Duncan was too used to her by now and ignored her glare. "Daphne was sensing something negative, but we couldn't figure it out at first because the only evidence was the nice ghost in room 202. And then he made his presence known. He threw my camera equipment—that really annoyed me because this stuff isn't cheap. But then he tried to possess Daphne and her internal battle with him caused her to pass out." Duncan shook his head. "It was crazy. But that day I learned never to underestimate Daphne when it comes to the paranormal. It could've gone so much worse that fateful day." He lit the leaves in the bowl and then said, "Okay, we're ready. Everyone sit in a circle and hold hands."

"Now?" Miguel asked, truly shocked. "In broad daylight?"

"Ghost stories are better in the dark," Duncan said, "but ghosts themselves are twenty-four-seven."

He patted the floor next to himself and Miguel had to exchange a look with Cayman. Was he the only one who really didn't want to sit on this dirty floor?

Cayman smiled and then sat down. "I'm willing to try anything. If after all these years some mysterious ghost wants to help us find Maddy, then so be it. I've done some wild things in my line of work."

"Stop being dramatic." Daphne rolled her eyes. "You worked cold cases. Miguel?"

He hesitated for a second, but then softened. Daphne needed this, he could see it in her eyes. If this was the way, it was worth sitting in whatever was on the floor. He'd just need to do a load of laundry later. Thank goodness he wasn't wearing his usual three-piece suit. When he sat, Daphne visibly relaxed and took the hand in the sling so she could be the one to gently hold where he was injured.

When they were all holding hands, Duncan said to Cayman and Miguel, "Now you two, hum."

"I'm sorry. Hum?" Miguel asked.

"Everyone has a job in a séance and since you two are new, you hum," Duncan instructed. "Usually, it's better with more people, but since we have a psychic present, we get a turbo boost."

"It unites you to the ceremony without having to know exactly what you're doing." Daphne was more direct. "It's very difficult for a spirit to resist when it is compelled." Her eyes got hard. "And I need to know who I'm dealing with."

Miguel felt ridiculous and fought the desire to ask if they actually believed this would work. But it was clear that they did, and he'd seen Daphne in action before, and it *was* truly unbelievable.

He started humming, "Row, Row, Row your boat," because it was the first thing that popped into his head and he was no singer. He wasn't looking for a tune with a challenge.

Cayman must've approved because he joined in. Miguel assumed that the former cold case detective was having similar doubts, but that he was also keeping them to himself. Likely, Cayman had also learned many years ago that Daphne's methods, no matter how unconventional, actually did work.

"Spirits of the world, we call on you." Duncan's eyes were closed as he spoke. Miguel looked around the circle and noticed everyone else's eyes were closed. He could only bring himself to squint.

"We know you walk among us," Duncan continued. "We ask that you now deliver to us the spirit who is connected to the Maddy Laurens disappearance. We call on you to deliver the spirit now."

"Spirit or spirits," Daphne added.

"Good call," Duncan said to Daphne. Into the circle he said, "We call on you to deliver any spirits connected with the Maddy Laurens disappearance now."

Duncan and Daphne stopped talking. They sat and waited.

"Do we keep humming?" Miguel asked. He had no idea what was supposed to be happening, but since nothing obvious *was* happening, the awkwardness of humming for no reason was getting to him.

"Yes," Duncan explained calmly. "Sometimes it takes a bit."

"Don't stop!" Daphne blurted. She was sensing something and so added, "Spirits of the world, show yourselves!"

Miguel and Cayman continued humming as Duncan added, "We call on you to deliver the spirit or spirits who are helping Daphne. Now!"

A shimmer appeared in the circle above the metal bowl and tealights, and then it vanished again.

Daphne shouted forcefully, "Show yourself!" There was no confusion over what she wanted.

Whatever had been trying to appear now slowly began to manifest itself. At first it was more like distorted air. And then it was wavy like heat waves coming off the asphalt. But after a few seconds, the apparition was very clear.

Floating before them was a young woman. Cute, blonde, petite.

And even though she was completely harmless looking, Miguel scrambled back from the circle at the sight. He'd never seen a ghost materialize before.

And then he felt silly for his reaction and tried to play it cool, but he still got a side-eye from Cayman.

"Could this lady be related to Maddy Laurens?"

Duncan asked.

But Daphne shook her head emphatically. "No, she's not related to Maddy Laurens at all."

"But that's what we summoned. Whoever is helping you," Duncan responded.

"She might be helping me, I guess. But it doesn't make any sense," Daphne almost whispered, her mind was so focused on piecing every fragment together.

"Do you know who this is?" Miguel asked.

Daphne's face was all hard lines and intensity. She looked ready to explode at any moment. "Oh, yes. I know exactly who this is."

6.

"What are you doing here, Grandma?" Daphne demanded.

"Grandma?" Miguel couldn't help the shock that blurted out. "Is this *your* grandma? Or Maddy's?"

"Maddy's grandmothers are both alive and well," Cayman explained. He looked from Miguel to Duncan to Daphne, as if the answer to the mystery of who this was would be written on their foreheads.

"She's mine," Daphne explained, her face as hard as rocks.

"Great!" Duncan squeezed Daphne's hand as he smiled. "Your grandma is helping you. This is perfect."

"It's not perfect." Daphne spoke clipped words through tight lips.

"Why is she young?" Miguel asked.

"Why are you mad?" Duncan asked.

"Is she *not* helping?" Cayman asked, still looking around at the small circle of people around him.

Daphne ignored them all.

She spoke directly to her grandma, asking again, "What are you doing here, Grandma Jean?"

Grandma Jean moved her lips, her face soft and gentle toward her grown granddaughter.

"She's saying something," Cayman shouted. Far louder than was necessary, Daphne felt.

"I didn't hear anything." Miguel, who was on the other side of the spirit, couldn't see the front of the ghost.

Duncan leaned in to explain to Daphne's new-to-paranormal boyfriend, "Sometimes it takes too much energy for multiple senses to come through. You can see them, or hear them, or feel a cold spot or something, but for them to reach all three senses at once is too much." He turned to Daphne. "Unless you're a medium or something."

"She's spouting bullshit anyway." Daphne glared

at her grandmother's ghost.

"I can't stay long," the ghost of Jean Winters said to Daphne. "Hear me out before I have to leave."

"We compelled you," Daphne argued. "You have to stay."

"This isn't about Maddy. It never has been." Jean had kind eyes and a sweet smile. She appeared before them as an adorable young lady, dressed in the finest clothing the 1970's had to offer: bell bottom jeans, striped halter top, large hoop earrings with feathered hair. Jean Winters had always cared about fashion, make-up, glitz and glamour. She'd had dreams of being a movie starlet, but she had never reached much beyond dating around with various Hollywood moguls.

Daphne hated that about her.

She'd never had her priorities straight—and life was precious. In Daphne's opinion, Jean had wasted all she'd been given chasing vapid, useless dreams. And then she died.

"I'm not here to talk about our relationship,

Grandma Jean," Daphne continued arguing. She wasn't yelling—yet. But she was dangerously close, her anger a toxic cocktail simmering just below the surface. Daphne had many talents, but subtlety and passivity had never been a strong suit. She didn't want distractions. She wanted answers. "Tell me who is helping me with Maddy."

"You have to let go first," Jean Winters' ghost explained.

When she added no further explanation, Daphne demanded, "What the hell are you talking about? Let go of what?"

"It's about you, Daphne. It's always been about you." Jean touched Daphne's cheek with the tenderness of someone who loved her. When she was alive, she was never a tender, loving grandmother. She'd been energetic, vivacious, larger-than-life, but not doting. Afterlife had given her the clarity that had eluded her in life, but the caring side of Jean Winters surprised Daphne, and she physically recoiled from her grandmother's touch.

Miguel, Cayman and Duncan all watched carefully,

eager to hear from Daphne what was really going on. They saw a loving grandmother—even if she did look twenty-five—and a granddaughter who resisted the love.

When Jean Winters reached out a second time, she was able to place a gentle palm on Daphne's cheek. And while Daphne was tense, she didn't pull away. When she felt her grandmother's touch, she saw an image in her mind as if her grandmother knew of no other way to get through to her.

A little girl. Two blonde pigtails. Seven or eight years old. She was running and crying, trying to find a place to hide as large, thundering footsteps echoed behind her. Someone was chasing her.

"No!" Daphne shook her head, trying to chase the image from her mind. It was wrong. It was all wrong. The innocence stolen. The monster in the shadows. The little girl in pigtails. "No, you're wrong!"

The ghost of Jean Winters smiled again, but instead of comforting Daphne it was annoying her. Now it felt like ridicule. Like this was all one big joke. "You've never needed a spirit guide for this one, Daphne. Do as you've always done and trust your intuition, even when it goes in dark places. That's how you'll find Maddy."

Her spirit began to grow brighter and brighter, until it filled the tiny, dirty apartment with rays as bright as the sun. And then, in a flash, the light was gone and so was Grandma Jean.

"Well, she's gone," Duncan announced.

"What just happened? Did you get what you needed, Daph?" Miguel was unsure what to say, completely clueless as to the events he had just witnessed. Yes, he knew she communicated with spirits, but he'd always just had to trust her before. This time he *saw* the interaction—and it still made no sense to his brain.

Daphne stood, folding her arms across her chest, a murderous look upon her face. "That was a colossal waste of time."

"You never know what you're going to get with a séance. I've never had any two go the same," Duncan said, blowing out the tealights and cleaning everything up.

"What exactly happened?" Miguel asked again.

Cayman watched Daphne, paying close attention to the silence. He stood next to her, a defiant pose to match her own. "A waste of time? Or did you just not like what you heard?"

Daphne stared down the hall of Duncan's apartment, too afraid to look at Cayman. His cop's intuition was far too keen.

"How could someone's own grandma tell them something they don't want to hear?" Miguel was genuine in his confusion.

But Daphne snapped at his ignorance. "You think because your abuelita is a sweet little old lady that everyone's grandmother is a saint? Mine was a fame whore on her best days."

"Enough with the aspersions, Daphne. What did she tell you?" Cayman was more aggressive than Miguel had seen him be yet. It was as if a switch had been flipped and he'd gone from retired to interrogation officer in two seconds flat.

"She said it was all about me. And that no spirit is helping me, I'm just not trusting my instincts," Daphne scowled.

"So, that's good, right?" Miguel looked from Daphne to Cayman to Duncan. Someone had to agree.

Daphne didn't respond so Cayman felt the need to translate her body language. He knew people like her all too well. And she wasn't even as guarded as she thought she was. "Clearly Daphne and her grandmother are not on the same page. But tell us everything, please." It was an instruction. His voice was clear and strong.

Daphne had never seen this side of Cayman. She knew he had a reputation as a tough cop, and he was a big man with a commanding presence. But none of that scared her at all. There wasn't much in this world that could scare her.

But it did surprise her.

He had always been reverent toward her, deferring to her skills, letting her lead the way at times. Something about his tone softened her resolve.

She stared at her feet as she spoke. "She put an image in my mind of a young girl hiding from someone trying to hurt her."

"Maddy," Miguel filled in the blank.

But Daphne shook her head. When she took too long to confirm or deny, Cayman prodded, "Daphne."

"It makes no sense. I'm telling you it's not helpful," Daphne shouted.

"Why would your grandmother show you an image that wasn't helpful, Daphne?" Duncan asked as he lifted the black bag where he kept his equipment. "I've worked with you on many cases and every little thing you've ever seen or felt has been helpful in some way. You yourself told me that only evil spirits have a reason to trick the living."

Shit. He was right.

Suddenly the room felt very small, the air thick. Were the walls actually closing in? She sat on the dirty couch and took deep, slow breaths. The weight of the reality was crashing in all around her and she wasn't sure where she'd be found within the rubble.

"Who was the girl, Daphne?" Cayman asked, his voice much less aggressive now, gentle even. He knew. She knew he knew. Of course, he did.

Daphne sighed. "Me." It was time to come clean. "The girl running from the bad man in the vision was me when I was eight years old."

7.

"The same age Maddy was when she was taken," Miguel realized. "That can't be a coincidence."

"Daphne." Duncan sat next to her on the couch. He was the most nurturing of the bunch and his intuition told him she needed someone at this moment. He might be a big guy, but he was gentle and kind. And Daphne had always been a friend to him. He'd seen past her rough exterior and blunt language from the day they'd met.

And she'd always loved that about him.

But she wasn't going to start being a softie now. The vision made no sense and nothing her grandmother said was useful. And that was the hill she was planning to die on.

"I'm sorry I wasted your time, Duncan," Daphne said, and she meant it.

"Nonsense. I haven't had a good séance in a while. I was sorta missing calling the ghosts to me instead of the other way around."

Cayman still stood with his arms folded across his chest. "What happened to you when you were eight, Daphne?"

"Nothing did."

Cayman scowled as they stared hard at each other. "I don't believe you."

"It doesn't really matter what you believe, Winston. I'm telling you, the vision was useless and this was all a waste of time." Daphne's face was hard as stone and left no more room for discussion.

So Miguel changed tactics. "Then we talk to the serial killer. Let's go."

But Cayman and Daphne didn't move. They continued their staring contest.

"Is the pickaxe vision real?" Cayman taunted.

Daphne stuck out her chin. "Of course."

"Why is one more real than the other?" Cayman

matched her body language. In the who-is-more-stubborn contest these two were a tie.

"Because. I just know the difference, Winston!" Daphne shouted at him. The frustration with her grandmother. The frustration with the case that made no sense. Her annoyance at Cayman not giving up. Her emotional barricade could take it no longer and she erupted. "Are you a psychic now? You know how to interpret visions and messages from spirits? No, you don't."

As if Daphne hadn't been speaking rhetorically, Cayman responded. He wasn't matching her shouting, but it was clear his own frustrations were bubbling to the top. "It doesn't take psychic abilities to see that you're full of crap. There's something you're not telling us." He softened his voice a bit to add, "Everyone in this room cares about you, Daphne. Why aren't you being honest?"

Daphne's chest exploded with the heavy breaths she was taking. She said nothing but looked at his dumb, round caring face. She knew he felt sorry for the girl in the vision. She didn't have to look at Miguel to know he would be concerned, also. And their pity was making her nauseous. She shot pure anger from the scowl on her face.

And then she ran out the front door of the apartment.

"You know,"—Duncan walked to the hallway closet and plopped the bag on the floor unceremoniously.—"Daphne is rarely under a microscope in a good way. Can't be easy. When I was growing up, everyone always judged me by my size. They were mad when I couldn't play football or basketball. What kind of freak is blessed with God-given size and then sucks at sports?" Duncan shrugged as if only God himself could possibly know. "Being judged all the time, ostracized by your community, abandoned by your family. It's gotta be exhausting."

Duncan had only been stating facts, but both Cayman and Miguel felt like they'd been reprimanded.

"Maddy Laurens has been missing for twenty-seven years. Her family has had no answers, no closure.

Sometimes to get answers, things have to get a little bit uncomfortable," Cayman said, defending himself. He never wanted to hurt Daphne, but he also felt there was something she was keeping from him and it bothered him immensely.

Miguel sighed. He'd had some interesting adventures with Daphne in their short time together, but imagining her as a victim had never entered his mind before now. If any part of the vision was real, then Daphne had also been wronged for many years. And Duncan was right—it had to be exhausting.

"Nice meeting you, Duncan." Miguel shook the big paranormal investigator's hand and followed Daphne out the front door.

She wasn't too hard to find. She hadn't gone far. She was back at the front gate to the apartment complex, staring at some graffiti on the wall. Her mind was elsewhere.

Miguel rarely knew what to say around Daphne. He found her fascinating and beautiful and intelligent. But he had moments when the fact that he understood about one percent of her world would hit him very hard.

This was one of those times.

So he stood next to her and joined her in staring at the graffiti. It was written in bubbly letters with green spray paint, and someone had taken the time to create highlights in a very artistic way. It looked like maybe they were trying to write "Angel" but it was written "Angll." Miguel wondered privately who Angll was around here.

"He's just a kid," Daphne answered his unvocalized thoughts. "He wants to be tough, like he's in a gang, but really he's just a kid with a tough home life and a dark future."

Miguel smiled. Putting an arm around her shoulder, he pulled her in and kissed her forehead. "Ladies and gentleman, she's still got it."

Daphne snorted. "I'm only blocked when it comes to Maddy Laurens. And I can't figure out why. And I have no idea why my grandmother would waste our time with distractions. It's very frustrating."

"I know you aren't close with your family, but do you become closer when they die?"

Daphne shook her head. "I never tried. It wasn't that I harbored any ill feelings or anything. I just never cared. My family is old Hollywood. Grandma Jean, the nice ghost you just met, had three husbands and they were all film directors or producers. My grandfather was husband number two. And their son? My father? Beck Winters, the famous director."

Miguel couldn't hide his shock and awe. "Whoa! Beck Winters is your dad?"

Daphne rolled her eyes. "And this is why I never tell anyone."

"So you grew up a Hollywood brat? But you hate movies." Miguel tried to wrap his brain around a young Daphne growing up around movie stars and running through mansions in the Hollywood Hills.

He couldn't do it.

And Daphne gave him a look. "No, I grew up a Hollywood outcast. Everyone around here loves to keep their secrets. It's like a contest of who could be the most full of shit. Only it never worked with me. I knew all their secrets. And it never earned me any special places in their hearts."

As he exited the apartment gate, Cayman cleared his throat to let them know he was there. He wasn't going to apologize—asphalt would crumble before that day occurred—but he did have the decency to look a tiny bit contrite.

And anyway, Daphne had never needed words. She knew.

She knew he was like a dog with a bone when it came to solving a case. She knew he hadn't gotten a perfect record in cold cases by pussyfooting around people's feelings. She knew he never meant to hurt her. That was just a side effect. And she'd already moved past his accusations. It was time to focus on Maddy.

"I have to say, I did like the movie *Searchlight*. It was one of the things that inspired me to become a cop." Miguel felt the need to tell everyone. To clarify to Cayman he added, "Did you know her dad is the director Beck Winters?"

Cayman raised an eyebrow at Daphne but said nothing. He'd lived in Southern California long enough to know that the term "Old Hollywood" wasn't always a compliment.

Daphne put a hand on her hip. "Is this going to be a thing now? I haven't seen my dad in years. The reason Duncan is my new family"— She aimed a thumb up at the decrepit apartment building.—"is because he never judges me."

"Can we stay focused? No one here cares about your rich, asshole father, Daphne." Cayman leaned against the worn-down building and Miguel hoped it wouldn't crumble beneath him. "We're no closer to finding who killed Maddy so we need to go back to the pickaxe."

Miguel pointed at him. "The serial killer in Arizona." He turned to Daphne. "You're with two detectives. You don't need to solve everything in the spirit world. Take a break this case and join us the old-fashioned way."

"His name is Rex Sutton. Mean, white supremacist style S.O.B." Cayman shook his head. "Said he used a pickaxe on his victims because it was a more perfect form of torture—violent but slow."

Daphne rolled her eyes. "He sounds delightful."

A man dressed in torn clothes, pushing a shopping cart and smelling like showers were an unknown luxury, stumbled past muttering to himself.

"Seriously. How does Duncan live here?" Miguel watched the homeless man pass. "This building needs to be bulldozed."

Daphne shrugged. "You met him. Things moving on their own? Footsteps echoing in an empty house? Evil spirits and voodoo? Duncan stops everything and pays attention. Anything else? He's ambivalent."

Miguel slipped his hand into Daphne's and squeezed. At the very least he was learning more about her this trip and he loved that. "Duncan seems like a good guy. I can see why he's like a brother to you."

"Duncan seems like a real peach, but we lost a lot of time with Hollywood Grandma in there." Cayman pushed off the wall, his broad chest leading the way for the rest of his body. "If we're done with distractions, I'd like to hit the road for Arizona."

"We're too late to talk to Rex Sutton today, but if we crash there, we can talk to him first thing in the morning," Miguel added. Séances and ghosts? He was useless. But this? This was the world he knew. He could add value to this phase of the plan.

"All right you two meatheads." Daphne shook her head, her bleached blonde spikes staying ramrod straight as she did. "You can interrogate, but I am searching for the truth. Hopefully I am not blocked with him like other aspects of this case. I want to know what happened to Maddy and where we can find her now."

Cayman and Miguel nodded. The truth was all any of them were searching for. On that they were very much aligned.

"I'll drive," Cayman announced, and the car

beeped as he unlocked it. They had a long drive ahead.

"Can't wait to see how this guy reacts to me," Miguel said. He and Cayman chatted casually as they got in the car.

But Daphne didn't move. A vision popped into her head of a little girl with pigtails. And blood. So much blood. She was crying and drenched in blood. What *was* that? She couldn't make the pieces fit.

"You coming, Daph?" Miguel called out with a smile, his perfectly gelled hair framing his handsome face. Nothing was ever out of place with Miguel. It both annoyed and comforted her.

She plastered on an overzealous grin. "Yes, of course. Can't wait to talk to the pickaxe serial killer human garbage asshole." And she climbed in the car.

This time, she kept the vision and its frustrating lack of clarity completely to herself.

8.

The maximum-security prison in Florence, Arizona, gave Daphne the chills before they'd even entered the building. As a child, she'd learned to control visits from unwanted spirits out of pure necessity. You can't live with ghosts constantly trying to talk to you. It's really hard to play dolls with the other little girls while a spirit nags you.

But the emotions.

Daphne still struggled with keeping the emotions at bay. And they were flooding her senses now. Jealousy. Frustration. Rage. Loss. Pain. They flew at her, stabbing her like a thousand knives.

Without realizing it was happening, Daphne winced. Miguel ran to her side, but she waved him off. Sometimes his need to shield her could drive her crazy.

"I'm okay. Just have to steel myself for the vibe of this place."

"No matter how many times you enter a prison, it still sucks every time." Cayman stretched his back as he stared at the gray prison walls.

"Sheer poetry, Winston. You should make the switch from fishing." Daphne rolled her eyes.

Winston smiled with mischief twinkling in his eye. "There once was a prison that sucked..."

Miguel added, "Where all of its people were fucked."

"Okay, okay. I don't need to hear any more of this crap. The prison itself is already making me nauseous. I don't need your limericks to really make me lose my breakfast." Daphne marched toward the front entrance without looking at the men, who were laughing at their own cleverness.

After checking in and leaving all weapons at the front, they were escorted down a long, barren hallway. It was colder than anywhere Daphne had ever been before.

It was as if despair had drained the hallway of the last hope you had when you walked in the front. Daphne shivered in response.

The room they were led to wasn't private, but it was early enough in the day that there was only one other prisoner talking to someone at a table in a corner. The woman not in an orange jumpsuit was dressed to the nines, and Daphne knew on instinct that she was his lawyer. They spoke quietly and intently.

Cayman, Miguel and Daphne all sat at a long table facing a secure door that led to the prisoners' holdings. Windows were reinforced with wire. Walls were thick and solid. Armed guards stood watch every six feet. This was not a place for petty crimes.

The clock seemed to tick so slowly, the seconds stretched until they snapped forward in time. Daphne watched the prison door until it buzzed. She shifted uncomfortably in her seat, bracing herself for the sight of the pickaxe murderer.

Rex Sutton. What a douchebag.

The first thing that struck Daphne as he entered the room was how tiny he was. Sizing him up, she judged that in hand-to-hand combat—without a pickaxe in his hand of course—this man couldn't do anything to her. She knew she was taller than the average woman, but nothing about this man at face value was intimidating.

But she could read his soul. And that was rancid.

Daphne swallowed hard as his hatred for the world rushed toward her, emanating from the tiny man. He winked at her as he sat down. He knew he made her uncomfortable and he relished that. There was only so much to entertain him these days, and watching a woman squirm in her seat when he entered the room was pure gold.

In return, Daphne made her face as impassive as she could.

Her instinct to tell this man to take a flying leap was exactly the reaction he wanted, so she fought the urge.

"To what do I owe this pleasure?" Rex Sutton

smiled with all the warmth of a predator lying in wait. "Two detectives and a cute lady? It's more than I could have dreamed up."

Daphne cemented herself to her seat—because what she really wanted to do was reach across the table and slap his face until her hand was sore, and she knew that would be counter-productive.

Miguel gestured at Rex, implying that Daphne and Cayman should lead the questioning. Even though their investigation was completely unofficial, it was still more their case than Miguel's. He was just along for the ride while his shoulder healed.

And Cayman and Daphne had been partners for a while, so he knew she would let him drive the interrogation while she popped in with things she knew to be untrue or any direction she was sensing.

"Rex. I'm Detective Cayman and this is Detective Alvarez and Daphne Winters, a psychic investigator with the LAPD," Cayman explained.

"I know who you are" Rex Sutton winked at

Daphne again and she swallowed her nausea in response.

"We're here about a missing girl named Maddy Laurens," Cayman started.

Rex Sutton leaned in, his sinewy arms resting on the table. "Never heard of her."

"She died in 1997, brutally attacked by a man with a pickaxe." Cayman said the words slowly, purposefully, letting the word pickaxe do all the work.

Rex flashed teeth with an evil grin. "I admire his craftsmanship."

Daphne would have been annoyed by his smug attitude, but she was distracted by the spirits entering the room. There were seven women standing behind him. As she'd heard was typical with serial killers, he had a type. Each young victim had long brown hair, was petite, young and pretty. And covered in blood, hair matted with sticky red. Daphne knew these were Rex Sutton's victims, haunting him in their afterlife. Sadly, he probably enjoyed the attention, even if it was from ghosts.

"This is Maddy Laurens." Cayman pulled out the

picture of her, a smiling young girl with a twinkle in her eye and all the happiness of a carefree young life staring back at the camera.

"Nope. Not mine." Rex lifted his chin but didn't even look at the photo.

Cayman was getting frustrated but he took a deep breath to calm his demeanor. There was a time to get rough with a suspect, but he was no where near that point yet. "This girl." He held the photo in front of Rex's face so he'd have to see her picture. "She was killed with a *pickaxe*."

"I ain't no child murderer," Rex sneered.

Miguel leaned in. "Okay but maybe you know someone? Or something that can help us?"

Rex looked at Cayman, completely ignoring Miguel's existence. "I don't talk to Mettzicans. And I have no idea why I'd help you even if I did."

Miguel tensed at the racism, but he forced himself not to react. He'd dealt with it all his life and the list was long of suspects and culprits that didn't take too kindly to being arrested and interrogated by a Hispanic policeman. It didn't make it less obnoxious, but he could compose himself. He could rise above it.

Daphne, on the other hand, was not used to racism and had very little tolerance for bullies. She stood and glared at the killer across the table. "Oh, yeah? You're half the man Miguel is, you hunk of shit. While you rot in here playing boyfriend to men twice your size, he's out there fighting for victims of people like you. He's a hero."

Rex Sutton curled his lip in delight. It had been a while since he'd seen a woman all tense and angry, and it satiated a craving in his depraved heart. "You a psychic? What am I thinking right now?"

His thoughts were heaped in more death, but Daphne didn't allow herself to be sucked into the trap. She stared at the ghosts of the women behind him instead, focusing her energy on their stories. The stories of the women whose lives he stole. Miguel rubbed her arm and gently pulled her back down into her seat.

Rex Sutton just laughed. The sound was hell itself.

"Where is Maddy Laurens? You tell us where her body is and we can work to help get your sentence reduced." Cayman continued his line of questioning, as if Daphne hadn't had an outburst. And as if he had any authority whatsoever to actually reduce someone's sentence.

"You can get me out of here?" Rex Sutton suddenly perked up, his whole demeanor changing. Originally, entertaining these detectives was just something to do. A way to pass the interminable time behind bars. But reducing his sentence? Well, that changed things.

"Forget it, Cayman." Daphne spit the words. "I can see his victims. They follow him everywhere he goes." She was staring up and over Rex's shoulder, so on instinct he turned behind himself to see the ghosts. He saw nothing. "He was telling the truth the first time. He didn't kill Maddy."

"What the hell, Daphne?" Cayman was annoyed at the derailment of the interrogation. He didn't appreciate her tipping their hand, even if it was the truth.

"I buried her in the desert. Out near Kearney. Get me a map and I'll show you." Rex Sutton's body language had gone from smug to desperate. He couldn't let the investigators out of this room now without a chance at freedom.

"He's lying. You'll waste time digging where there's no body." Daphne leaned back in her seat and folded her arms.

"Why don't you ask my *ghosts*?" Rex was laughing at her, making fun. He obviously didn't believe they were really there in the room.

"You have seven victims, not just the six you were charged with. The first woman, Maggie, took three days to die because you were sloppy and new. You didn't know what you were doing. Every night when you sleep, she watches you, pushing on your chest to make it difficult to breathe." Daphne looked at the ghosts behind him. "Yes, I think Maggie hates you the most of all."

Instinctively, Rex rubbed his chest and then said,

"You know everything about me. That's super sexy."

It was Miguel's turn to shoot up out of his chair. You could say whatever you wanted to about him and he'd remain calm and steady. But comments about Daphne? It drove straight to the core.

"Ah," Rex grinned. "Protective of your lady, I see." He turned to Daphne. "Call off your dog, lady friend."

"Shut up!" Miguel shouted at the same time Daphne blurted, "Go to hell!"

"Okay." Cayman stood up and waved his arms, diffusing the situation before it went more off the rails. "If you know for a fact he didn't kill Maddy, Daphne, then we're done here."

"No, I can help you," Rex said again, but there was less conviction in his tone this time around.

Daphne stood and leaned across the table, her hands placed in the middle to prop herself up as she got in Rex's tiny little smug face. "You can't help anyone. You never could. The thing is, Rex, your mother was right all along. You're a complete mistake in this world. But those girls?" She pointed at the ghosts behind him that only she could see. "They were good and special with hopes and dreams to share. You didn't just kill them. You punched a hole in the balance of the universe. So, no, you can't help us at all. But I can help those girls find the peace they deserve. And when I'm done? I'm finding Maddy Laurens. And you can rot in hell."

"I so badly want a pickaxe right now," Rex muttered, but in a way that conveyed reverence. He was in awe of Daphne and it continued as she walked around the table toward the ghosts of his victims.

"Ma'am, you need to stay on the other side of the table." A security guard moved forward, blocking Daphne's path with his arm.

"I'm just helping his victims find closure," Daphne explained, pushing forward against his arm. But it was futile. This guy was strong.

"Who?" The guard looked around but saw nothing and had no idea what she was talking about.

"Officer, we're done here," Cayman announced,

deciding the best course of action was to get Rex Sutton out of here. The security guard grabbed Rex's arm and pulled him up out of his seat. The whole time he exited, Rex was watching Daphne in fascination. She, in turn, was watching the women whose lives Rex Sutton had cut short with a pickaxe.

"Daphne, let's go. We have a long drive ahead of us." Miguel reached across the table for her hand, but she pulled away.

"I have to do this." While she centered herself for the spiritual reading, Cayman and Miguel sat back down to let her have her moment. The other prisoner and his lawyer looked up for a moment, but deciding she was just a weirdo, they went back to their conversation.

Daphne reached both her hands out, grabbing hands with the spirit of Maggie, Rex's first victim, and Jennifer, his last. "It's time, ladies. You don't need to spend your eternity throwing out the garbage. He'll get what's coming to him. And you deserve to rest."

The ceiling opened up and a thick ray of light

appeared right next to where they were standing. Daphne had seen this many times before. Their ride was here, ready to take them home. Daphne gestured to the light with her chin so the spirits of Rex Sutton's victims would know where it was. "Here you go. This is for you. Time for some peace."

At the word "peace" a few of the women looked calm and ready to go. They started to head toward the light. Except Jennifer was still holding Daphne's hand. "I'm not sure I'm ready to stop watching him. I don't trust him." She frowned as she spoke.

Daphne squeezed Jennifer's hand. She could certainly understand not trusting a man like that. Besides, Jennifer had first-hand knowledge of what this man was capable of. But Daphne wasn't here for Rex Sutton's rehabilitation. She cared only for the souls of his victims. And she knew Jennifer was ready.

Daphne began leading Jennifer to the light where the other ghosts had already gone. "You don't have to trust him. He's not your burden." She had more to say, but before she could verbalize any more words of encouragement for Jennifer, a vision popped into Daphne's head.

A young girl with blonde pigtails, covered with so much blood it looked like paint. She was running. And crying. Every few feet she would look behind her. And Daphne felt the fear. The terror, actually. She was overwhelmed by it, and Daphne fell to the floor of the prison, the weight of the terror holding her down. Tears were streaming from her eyes and all she could see was a terrified little girl running toward a woman with outstretched arms.

Daphne knew that woman. What the hell?

"Daphne? Are you okay?" Miguel was at her side, kneeling next to her, one arm around her shoulder in comfort.

Daphne looked up at him, confused for a second how she got back here in the room where they had just talked to a serial killer. She said nothing but realized she was still crying and wiped the tears from her cheeks. She was embarrassed by the emotions. And embarrassed by what she saw. Even though Miguel had no idea what that was.

"Where's Jennifer?" Daphne asked, looking around. The light was gone and so were all the ghosts.

"Who's Jennifer?" Miguel asked, looking around in imitation of Daphne, knowing full well he couldn't see what she could see anyway.

Daphne stood, suddenly angry. She hadn't finished the job. Stupid vision had interrupted her. "She was right here. Afraid to go into the light because she wanted to protect other women from Rex Sutton. Did she cross over?"

Daphne was looking at Miguel but the question was really meant more for herself.

He shook his head. "I don't know."

Cayman grabbed Daphne's hand and propelled her toward the exit. "She crossed over. Your work here is done." He didn't actually know that, but he didn't want to spend any more time helping ghosts on a case they *weren't* working.

And Daphne knew what was happening, but she appreciated it anyway. She really wanted to leave this room, as if that would distance her somehow from the vision in her mind.

They collected their belongings at the front desk and Cayman stared at his phone in confusion. "Huh. Detective Dalton called." He marched out the front door to call him back.

Miguel walked slowly with Daphne, who kept peering over her shoulder. The vision haunted her more than any ghosts ever had. The emotions from the little girl in the vision were so heavy they pulled her shoulders down physically like some unseen anchor.

"You sure you're okay?" Miguel didn't know what to ask. He had no idea what she'd seen but he knew it was bothering her.

And Daphne was thankful he didn't pry. It was one of the things she loved about him. "Yeah," she lied.

They stepped through the main entrance door into

the bright Arizona sun. The contrast from the gloomy prison was sharp and they were momentarily blinded. Cayman met them at the front with a sour face.

"Whatever tricks you have up your sleeve, I'm going to need you to whip them out pronto," Cayman instructed, his hands on his hips.

"Because?" Daphne asked. She hated being told what to do.

"LAPD Cold Cases is reopening the Maddy Laurens case. I have to hand over every file I have by 5 pm tomorrow." Cayman tightened his lips in frustration.

"I thought no one cared about this case anymore." Miguel re-stated the belief they'd been operating under since Cayman said it the morning prior.

"Apparently, someone made a big stink with the Chief and he actually listened for some unknown reason. So suddenly law enforcement cares again." Cayman kept his eyes locked on Daphne even as he answered Miguel. Rex Sutton was the lead to nowhere so they couldn't solve the case in a day without Daphne's extracurricular talents.

Daphne narrowed her eyes with annoyance. This case had haunted her for years, kept her up nights. And now, suddenly, it might be taken away? Not happening.

"Unfortunately, my latest vision gave me a clue of someone who might know something," Daphne scowled.

"That's great news." Miguel was the only thrilled person in their trio. "Who is it? Do we know?"

"Yeah, I know her." Daphne pouted and looked at no one. She couldn't make eye contact. "She's my mother."

9.

"We're on a clock now, Daphne. Everything's changed." Cayman pulled into the motel where Miguel and Daphne were staying. He stated the obvious as if Daphne hadn't spent the entire drive home from Arizona blaming herself for how this case had taken so long. Why couldn't she just see the face of Maddy's attacker? Why couldn't she sense where Maddy's remains were taken?

It didn't make any sense.

"If you knew my mom, you'd be hesitant too," Daphne muttered.

"I just don't get it. How can your mom possibly know what happened to Maddy?" Miguel asked.

Daphne shook her head. Everything with this case was a complete mystery to her. It was always just out of reach of her mind's eye. Just when she thought she had something to grab onto, it twisted into something new. A new puzzle piece that didn't fit the puzzle but somehow belonged. "All I know is, she was in my vision. She's involved somehow," Daphne said.

Cayman leaned over the seat to talk to Daphne. "I can talk to her if you want me to. You two just stay here and I'll see what I can find out."

Daphne started chewing on a fingernail. She'd never had that habit before, but then again, she'd never not known conclusively what her visions meant. The bewilderment was giving her anxieties she'd never felt before. "I think I have to be there. To know the things you can't hear with your ears."

Cayman nodded. "I get that. So let's go tonight. I have to hand over the files tomorrow and then we are truly an obstruction to justice if we keep working on it." Cayman stated the obvious yet again.

"We don't have to go tonight if you don't want to, Daph." Miguel rubbed her arm with his good hand.

She sighed in response. When did she get to be such a wimp? Afraid of her own mother? She confronted ghosts, demons, murderers, the things everyone else was afraid of. But her own family terrified her more than any of that combined.

She'd never had much luck with the living.

"Fine. We can go now." Daphne pointed at Cayman. She knew Miguel would support her and let her lead, but Cayman was too much of a cop not to step in and interrogate. "But *I'm* doing all the questioning. You don't even know what you're asking her about."

"Neither do you," Cayman responded. Daphne couldn't deny it, but she didn't want to say the words out loud, so she ignored him. He started the car and pulled out of the parking lot, heading toward the windy canyon that would take him out to Malibu where Alanna Savage lived on a cliff overlooking the ocean.

When it came to Daphne, Miguel was more intuitive than he gave himself credit for. Without even knowing Alanna Savage outside of the tabloids, he was nervous on Daphne's behalf. "When is the last time you saw your mother?"

Daphne looked at her hands. "Ten years." She hated the house in Malibu. The second she was able to earn a living, she had bolted and never looked back. Growing up with the Hollywood crowd, and the kids of stars, surrounded by everyone who'd "made it," Daphne had always just felt like a shoe on the wrong foot. A roach in the cheesecake. A blemish on the landscape.

As far back as she could remember, she'd been planning to escape.

If you weren't a pro at the canyon roads, you would have to take them very slowly. And luckily Cayman wasn't, so the twists and turns were leisurely, and still Daphne wished he'd go slower.

She took a deep breath to steady herself. She reminded herself that this was her mother. The woman who had given her life. There was nothing to be nervous about.

It wasn't working. She was still dreading the

encounter.

"Alanna Savage and Beck Winters. With that pedigree, people would expect you to want to be in the film industry somehow." Miguel spoke his thoughts aloud. He didn't really care that much about Hollywood, but it was still pretty amazing.

Daphne snorted. "Until you meet me."

Miguel squeezed her hand. "It's just something you don't hear every day. That's all."

Daphne squeezed his hand in return. She could sense his surprise at her connection to two famous Hollywood legends and knew that it was just that— surprise and nothing more. "Believe me, no one knows because I don't want them to know. Growing up, there was an absolute expectation of what I should be. And I never was. Love me or hate me, I want it to be because of what I bring to the table and not who my parents are. Or what dumb movies they made."

"No one wants to be judged by their parents," Cayman said as he rounded another corner. They came up over a hill and the ocean appeared before them.

For Miguel, living in Fresno, the ocean was a rare commodity. Sure, he could drive three hours and see it, but he rarely did. There was always one more case, or more paperwork, or more skills to hone. He leaned forward to get a good view. "It's so beautiful out here."

Daphne watched Miguel enjoy the view. That meant more to her than the dumb ocean she'd seen a thousand times. In her mind, Fresno was home now and this was just a painful memory. Instead of admiring the views, she'd spent her whole childhood planning to leave.

Cayman pulled onto a narrow driveway and climbed slowly toward the crest of the hill. The home he parked his car in front of looked as if it were completely made of glass, with sharp lines and angles. Looking from the driveway, you could see the ocean right through the house. It was a far cry from the three-bedroom bungalow Miguel had grown up in.

Sensing Daphne's discomfort, Miguel kept his thoughts of how cool Alanna Savage's house was to himself.

Cayman, however, couldn't help himself. "Whoa. You grew up here? This place looks amazing."

She'd heard it all her life, so she just ignored him. To her this place was nothing but glass, stone and loneliness.

Climbing out of the car and slamming the door, Daphne announced, "Let's go find out what my mom knows." But she stood there in silence, looking up at the house, not daring to move forward. Miguel came around and rubbed her shoulder. It was moments like these he wished he were psychic too.

"She's just a person. You got this," Miguel whispered in her ear.

She knew these were words of encouragement, but they stung. Because she never wanted to be perceived as weak. Weird? Quirky? Fine. She embraced those descriptions. But afraid of her mother? She didn't want to let that show and she was annoyed he could see it so easily.

Rolling her shoulders back, she responded, "I know." And it was just as much to herself as to Miguel. Because her mother *was* just a person. And no one knew human flaws as well as Daphne. The truths of human frailty were revealed to her constantly.

She marched up to the front door and a flood of memories came back to her. It had been a decade since she'd stood on this doorstep, yet in so many ways it was like yesterday. Eating an ice cream cone that had dripped a path along this very walkway. Learning to ride a bike in the driveway where Cayman had parked. Walking through this door every day when she came home from school. So mundane, yet all a constant reminder of just how different Daphne really was and had always been.

She raised her hand to knock, but the door opened before her knuckles made a sound.

"My dearest, darlingest, daringest Daphne!" The woman's arms swooped open and grabbed an uncomfortable Daphne into an overbearing hug. It was so melodramatic a greeting that Miguel had to stifle a laugh.

Even without make-up and the glitz and glamour of the red carpet, Alanna Savage was stunning. And, sure, there was a resemblance between the two ladies. It was easy to see where Daphne got her good looks, but other than that these two women could not be more different from one another.

Where Alanna was poised and fancy, Daphne was salt of the earth. Where Alanna was flamboyant and over the top, Daphne was real and authentic.

Daphne patted her mother's back, but there was little warmth. She mostly looked uncomfortable.

When Alanna Savage was done embracing her estranged daughter, she pulled back and grabbed Daphne's chin. "Let me look at you." A scrutinizing eye scanned Daphne from head to toe. "Your skin still looks good. I see the regimen I taught you is still working well. But where is your hair? You look like a man." She reached to touch Daphne's hair and Daphne pulled back.

"Hi, Mom," Daphne said, her words laced with annoyance at her mother's judgment. It was always about looks with this famous actress.

Peering over Daphne's shoulder, Alanna asked, "Who are your gentlemen friends?" She flashed a smile that said she had used this trick before to have men grovel at her feet.

"They're homicide detectives, Mom. I help them solve murder cases."

Miguel reached out to shake Alanna's hand. "Detective Miguel Alvarez, ma'am." She smiled and gave Miguel a limp wrist. Miguel wanted to add that he was in love with Daphne, but he also didn't want to be the one to out their relationship to Daphne's estranged mother.

Alanna Savage turned her attention to Cayman, who did look somewhat smitten with the beautiful movie star standing in front of him. "And you are?"

Cayman cleared his throat to appear less nervous. "Detective Winston Cayman, Los Angeles P.D., Cold Case Division." And then he added, "Retired."

"Well." Alanna flashed one of the fakest smiles Miguel had ever seen. "It's lovely to meet you. And I couldn't be more thrilled to see my baby girl after all this time. But to what do I owe the pleasure of homicide detectives?"

"They're my friends, Mama. Relax." Daphne pushed past her mother and into the foyer of her beautiful childhood home. As if no time had passed, she marched to the living room and plopped on the oversized white couch. It was strategically placed to face the floor-to-ceiling windows that overlooked the ocean.

"So, it's a social visit? Can I get you anything to drink?" Without waiting for answers, Alanna waltzed into the kitchen that was open to the room Daphne was already sitting in. Cayman and Miguel followed hesitantly. They hadn't been formally invited in, but it was also weird to lurk in the doorway. They watched Alanna pour herself something strong from a fancy bottle and toss it back.

Daphne rolled her eyes. Some things never changed. "No. We won't be here long. Guys." She called Cayman and Miguel over to the couch. "Come sit."

Alanna refilled her glass and joined her

unexpected guests. She sat in a chair that angled toward the couch and placed a bare foot up on the coffee table. "So…. What have you been doing with yourself, Daphne? I want to hear all about it."

Daphne doubted very much that her mother cared one iota about what she'd been up to, but she needed information from her so she decided to play nice. "This. I help victims find closure by working with police departments to solve cold cases. Sometimes I work on paranormal cases and hauntings too."

Alanna sighed overdramatically. "Ghosts. Always ghosts. I had always assumed you'd outgrow that phase. Can't you do something real with your life?"

Miguel and Cayman tensed. They were witnessing a moment between a mother and daughter that they probably shouldn't be a part of.

"Says the woman who literally pretends to be made-up characters for a living." Daphne shook her head. She was never going to get her mom to understand. They were just too different. And although Daphne's instincts were to tell you how wrong you were and how little you knew about the real world, unfortunately she knew her mother too well. She didn't want to waste her time or her breath, so she directed the questioning back to the one thing she knew her mother would be happy to talk about: herself. "What have you been up to, Mother?"

Alanna's face lit up. She'd been hoping for this opening. "I should actually interview you detectives while I have you. I'm filming the pilot for a new crime scene show tomorrow called 'Clued In.' I'm really excited about it. I know it seems like I am downgrading by going from movie star to episodic television, but everyone is doing it these days. And you know what it's like for women of a certain age in Hollywood."

Daphne most certainly did not. Nor did she care.

"No one's going to judge you, Mom." Daphne rolled her eyes. Reputation and rumors were always the guiding light.

"Have you been to see your father?" Alanna leaned in, closing the distance between herself and

Daphne. It was clear by the look on her face that *she* wanted to see Daphne's father.

Miguel had no idea what the history was in the Winters household, but he imagined a tabloid headline of a famous director leaving his aging movie star wife for the newest young starlet from one of his films.

Daphne sighed. "No. I am sure he's busy." Daphne looked over to Cayman and Miguel. Cayman seemed content just to be in the presence of a beautiful actress, but Miguel nodded at Daphne, encouraging her to get to the point.

"Mom, we're here about a specific case."

Alanna had the good graces to look confused. Whether or not she was just using her superb acting skills, Miguel could only guess.

"We're trying to find the body and the killer of a young girl named Maddy Laurens who died in the 90's," Cayman said, leaning forward and rubbing his hands together, his initial excitement at being near a movie star giving way to business. Now that Daphne had gotten past the awkward reunion, he felt comfortable moving their reason for being here along.

"Well, that sounds terribly sad, but I have no idea what that has to do with me." Alanna sat up straight. She certainly didn't appear to be lying.

Fortunately, Daphne didn't need to try and read behavior like the detectives did. She knew intuitively that her mother was telling the truth.

Alanna Savage knew nothing of the murder of Maddy Laurens.

"I had a vision and you were there." Daphne physically shook her head as the pieces of this case continued to struggle to fit together. Why was she seeing things that had nothing to do with Maddy Laurens every time she thought about this case? "There was a little girl covered in blood. She had blonde pigtails." Daphne locked eyes with her mother. She pleaded with her silently to help make everything fit. "And she ran to you."

Alanna held her breath for a moment before saying, "You don't remember?"

Daphne concentrated. She locked in on her mother. On the vision. On Maddy Laurens. Searching for the truth amongst the emotions and visions she'd been having. The fragments collided with her conscience and she struggled to grasp anything solid.

There was something here. But it stopped her every time.

It pained her to say it, but she had no choice. For once, her God-given talents were failing her. "No. I don't know anything about what that vision means."

"That's because it's not a vision, Daphne." Alanna knelt before her daughter in a rare moment of tenderness. She placed a gentle hand on her daughter's knee. Her voice was soothing like a mother's should be. "It's a memory."

For some reason, Daphne turned to Miguel in this moment when the truth fell all around her. She was a psychic. She was in-tune with the world in a way no one else was. She saw things, felt things, *knew* things no one else did. But she didn't remember being covered in blood as a small child? Her eyes still locked on Miguel, she asked her mother, "Memory of what?"

She should have been afraid, but years of experience had told her to never be afraid of the truth. No matter what it was, she wanted to know. She *needed* to know.

Miguel sensed her discomfort and squeezed her hand.

"You almost died that day." Alanna smiled softly as she recounted the memory, filling in the details that Daphne couldn't in the way that a mother never forgets. "You were playing in the garage and you found your father's tools. He still lived with us at that time. You were maybe seven or eight. And for some reason, you chose to rifle through the tools. You dropped the pickaxe from above your head and it sliced the side of your face and went deep in your shoulder."

Alanna moved to sit next to her daughter on the couch, tears welling in her eyes. "We were at the hospital for hours. You had lost so much blood."

Daphne could tell her mother wasn't lying, but still this made no sense. "If I was cut so deeply, why do I not have any scars?"

Alanna put an arm around her daughter's shoulders. "Honey, I have all the best plastic surgeons on speed dial. And at that time, I still held onto the hopeless dream that you might follow in my footsteps onto the silver screen. I couldn't have you growing up with a nasty scar on your *face*."

"Do you remember any of this?" Miguel asked, concern lacing his eyes.

She hated it when people pitied her. She hated that more than anything. And especially for something she couldn't even remember. "No. But why would I block that out? It was just an accident." She was speaking aloud more to herself than anyone.

"And why was it a pickaxe?" Cayman brought it back to the Maddy Laurens case.

Daphne rolled her eyes. "You're not suggesting I killed her?"

"No, of course not." Cayman fought the urge to roll his own eyes. "But there's some connection there. Maybe your own pickaxe accident has been blocking you from the truth."

Daphne shook her head and stared at her hands. That wasn't it, was it? Has the whole reason she's been blocked in sensing Maddy Laurens been because she was injured by the murder weapon as a child? "No, that doesn't feel right."

"It's not unusual for childhood trauma to affect our psychology as adults. There may be a subconscious reason you've been blocking it all out. Perhaps it just hit too close to home." Miguel spoke gently, but it wasn't calming Daphne. He wasn't listening. He was back to coddling her. It was annoying her.

"It is called your 'psyche' for a reason," Cayman added as if it were a meaningful comment.

"Neither one of you is listening. This has nothing to do with Maddy Laurens. It was just something that happened to me as a kid." Daphne was on the threshold of losing her temper, and her hands shook as she attempted to keep her emotions bridled.

It came out before Miguel could decide if it was smart to push in this moment. "But how do you know? You can't sense anything whenever it comes to Maddy Laurens."

Daphne stood straight up. It might've been true—in fact, it probably was—but that didn't mean she had to like it. Everything shot to the top and boiled over. Miguel coddling her like she was a China doll as he had been this whole trip. Cayman insinuating there was a connection with the murder weapon. Her mother's mere self-absorbed presence. Her own lack of memory. The frustration over the Maddy Laurens case. The fact that *nothing* at all fit together in any meaningful way.

The fact that she couldn't sense the truth in this case the way she always did with her sixth sense.

She couldn't take any of it anymore.

"You're all wrong!" she screamed, her own voice sounding shrill and annoying even to her own ears. She couldn't care. "None of you are psychics so you don't know anything. Stop babying me, all of you! I wasn't traumatized as a child and I'm not a weakling."

Without waiting for a retort—the voice of reason that someone may present—she turned and ran out the front door. She knew she was being overtaken by emotions, but at this very moment she enjoyed the release. And she relished the fresh air outside the stifling childhood home where she was constantly smothered by the reminder of all her flaws.

Why couldn't she remember almost being killed by a pickaxe? And what was the connection to Maddy? In frustration, she kicked the closest thing she could find. A terracotta planter right outside the front door was the innocent victim.

Inside the living room with the ocean view, Daphne's outburst still left the air thick. Alanna Savage stood up and took a swig of her drink. On her stroll back to the kitchen she explained, "That's Daphne for you. All that actress blood running through her veins, no matter how she may try to deny it. Dramatic emotions have to have somewhere to go, or you burst and make any random place your stage."

Miguel stood, his desire to follow Daphne torn against his assumption that she could use a moment alone.

Cayman stood as well, but he was still focused on the prize. Daphne's little sideshow was just her denying what she didn't want to be true. Didn't make it false in his eyes, and it certainly wasn't going to dissuade him. He followed Alanna and also walked casually toward the kitchen. "Miss Savage, can you think of any reason why Daphne would be thinking about that childhood event in connection with the Maddy Laurens case?"

Alanna looked into the distance as she dug deep for the answer to his question. Whether it was because she truly wanted to help her daughter or because she just enjoyed being the center of their questioning, Cayman had no idea.

"Daphne was an odd little girl," Alanna frowned. "Imagine having anything a little girl could want. Clothes.

Dolls. Ice cream. Beck and I may not have been the best parents, but we gave her everything. And yet, all Daphne could talk about or think about were things that weren't even there. Ghosts, buried secrets, hidden emotions." Alanna sighed as she made eye contact with the husky detective. "It seems to me that perhaps the reason she can't get past this is because she never learned to process her own ghosts, buried secrets and hidden emotions. It's hard to look inward when you spend your whole life looking outward. Especially living in your own world that no one else understands."

Miguel remembered Duncan's words. *Daphne is rarely under a microscope in a good way. Can't be easy. Being judged all the time, ostracized by your community, abandoned by your family. It's gotta be exhausting.*

"Daphne may have been an odd child, but she's an amazing woman. If you stepped out of your own little bubble long enough to see the world through her eyes, you would know," Miguel said. He wasn't angry or judgmental, just stating facts.

Cayman pointed a thumb toward Miguel. "He's in love with her."

Alanna smiled. It warmed her heart to see this man who cared for Daphne defend her daughter's honor. "It would be a lie to say I never wished she'd stopped chasing ghosts, but I do think she's amazing. I never appreciated her when it mattered, but I do think she's pretty special." She turned to Cayman, resting a hand gently on his forearm. "Give her time. She'll work through whatever is holding her back. These are just waters she's never navigated before."

Cayman nodded even as he thought to himself about the fact that they were running out of time. They had exactly one day to hand over the case.

"Thank you for your time, Miss Savage." Cayman nodded his head as if to tip his imaginary hat. "And may I say that you are just as beautiful in person as you are in your movies."

Alanna Savage smiled. It still warmed her heart to get compliments from fans. "You may."

"Nice to meet you, Miss Savage," Miguel said to Daphne's mother. And it wasn't just words of formality—he truly meant it. Daphne so rarely spoke about where she grew up that it had been nice to meet someone from her childhood. "And if you ever find yourself in Fresno, stop by and say hi."

"I will," she said a little too enthusiastically.

They both knew she never would.

"And you take care of my daughter. She's tough, but it's mostly because she's covered herself in armor."

Miguel nodded and then Cayman got them back to the task at hand. "Armor that we need to dismantle in less than twenty-four hours or someone else is solving our case."

10.

Daphne was sitting in the car brooding.

Alanna walked Cayman and Miguel to the door and tossed a wave and blew a kiss at her daughter. Daphne ignored her. It was all for show anyway—the art of "playing" a good mother. And Daphne wasn't in the mood for theatrics right now.

She'd known since she was a kid that she was put on this earth to help people in a way that few people could. That communicating with the dead was important. It provided healing to those who'd lost loved ones. It gave comfort that they'd see their loved ones in the next life.

And it allowed Daphne to answer questions about how and why their loved ones had died as victims of violent crimes.

Her work *mattered.*

Alanna Savage on the red carpet wearing designer dresses could never understand that. Like most of Daphne's family, her mother's priorities were askew.

Coming here was a mistake.

Miguel climbed in the car and thankfully said nothing. If he'd opened his mouth to say one thing she probably would have snapped. Sometimes Miguel just understood her eerily well for someone she'd only known a short while.

"Do you remember when we first met?" Cayman asked as he climbed in the driver's seat.

Daphne just stared at him in response. They were no closer to solving Maddy's murder, running out of time, and he chooses now to reminisce?

"You were a skinny little thing. Your hair was jet black back then, too." Cayman laughed at the memory. "You were what? Nineteen?"

"Where are you going with this, Winston?" Daphne folded her arms across her chest in admonishment.

"But you were fierce, I'll give you that." He started the car. "I guess you were sick of the fluff and wanted to be a part of something real. I didn't know that at the time, but now it does make some sense why you showed up at my office when I didn't take your calls."

"That sounds familiar," Miguel whispered, but he was smiling as he did.

"Yeah. I wanted to use my gift in a meaningful way. What's so wrong with that?" Daphne was getting annoyed with Cayman, even though she knew he—like Miguel also—understood her exceedingly well. It made her uncomfortable to be surrounded by two men she couldn't really hide from.

Her usual barriers were fruitless against these two and it made her feel naked.

"Nothing. It's perfect." Cayman smiled at her in the rearview mirror.

"Why do you think we became cops?" Miguel added. "We all want the same thing. To see the bad guy get what's coming to him."

"I guess what I'm trying to say is, I see you, Daphne. This may be dark and ugly before it gets to the light, but Miguel and I know dark and ugly. Focus on *why* you want to solve this case instead of the pieces that hit so close to home. All three of us can handle whatever you're trying to hide."

Damn.

Daphne shifted in her seat. The exposure was getting to be too raw. She wanted to help others, but this was the first time it had been at her own expense.

Sensing where Cayman was going with this, Miguel added, "There's nothing you can tell us that changes anything, Daph. We all want the same thing: to find Maddy Laurens and bring her killer to justice. What do you know that you aren't sharing?"

Daphne could feel her blood boiling. Her anger had always been her defense mechanism. Keeping people at bay by scaring them off with anger, weirdness, and eccentricities. But in this case, she knew it would serve no purpose. Miguel was her soul mate and Cayman was as vested in Maddy's case as she was.

Daphne inhaled deeply as she looked to control her anger.

"Honestly, you guys." Daphne stared out the window as she spoke. "I don't know. I'm the little girl in my visions, my grandmother and mother both confirmed that. I'm covered in blood and hiding from someone trying to hurt me." She turned to look at Miguel. "But I don't remember it at all. And I don't have the first clue how it's related to Maddy."

Miguel's eyes were soft, but this time his look wasn't annoying her. When she stopped worrying about her own frustrations for a minute, she could sense that it wasn't pity. It was solidarity. He was on her side, always on her side.

She was so screwed up she hadn't even been able to see that.

When Miguel reached an arm out, she cuddled in close, seatbelt be damned. She'd never admit it out loud, but it felt soothing to get a good, old-fashioned hug.

"So you were a victim too?" Cayman spared a glance in the rearview mirror as he navigated the canyon roads.

Daphne shook her head. "I guess so, but it's so infuriating. I can't make sense out of anything I'm feeling. And this has never happened to me before. Usually I see *too* clearly. And with this? Nothing fits together."

"Okay. Well, let's start with what we do know." Miguel shifted to be able to look at her. "You were both young girls when you were victimized. And both injured by a pickaxe. That feels important somehow."

Daphne nodded. That much was true. "But I was living in Malibu and she was in the Valley, so two very different locations. How could it possibly be the same pickaxe?"

"Well, maybe it's not that you had the same attacker so much as the similarities you feel to Maddy's case are just clouding your psychic abilities because they bring up emotions and memories you don't want to face?" Cayman asked.

"So we need to get back on track on solving what's blocking you, and stop chasing the very limited clues about Maddy until we do," Miguel stated. His concern was always more about Daphne than Maddy anyway.

"Just one thing still isn't sitting right with me." Cayman wagged a pudgy finger as he spoke. "Your dad is a film director, right?"

"Yeah. And don't even bother trying to add him to the witness list." Daphne folded her arms. "Talking to him will be worse than talking to my mother."

"No, it's not that." Cayman shook his head. "I have a toolset. I use it every now and again too. It's got hammers, and screwdrivers. Heck, I even have a drill. But I am trying to think what home improvement project would require a pickaxe? What would a film director need one for in his tool chest?"

"Could your mom have been lying?" Miguel asked Daphne. "To try and cover up for your dad?"

"She told the truth as she knew it," Daphne responded. "Doesn't mean it's *the* truth, but she wasn't lying. I could sense that much."

Daphne dug deep, using the part of her brain that turned on so easily when she spoke to spirits. It was as natural for her as breathing. Was her father involved in Maddy's death somehow? Nothing. Instead of truth and clarity, what usually came at her in waves, she sensed nothing. But she knew her father. The rational side of her brain told her there was no way he could have done or known something.

He was domineering and vain, but he wasn't violent. In fact, Daphne got many of her traits about ignoring things she didn't like from her dad. He was more likely to run or hide from a problem than beat it with a pickaxe.

It didn't fit.

"How do we open up your gift? What can we do?" Miguel asked Daphne.

Daphne shrugged in response. "This is a first for me."

"Don't hate me, but I have an idea. And for some

reason I don't think you're going to like it," Cayman told the rearview mirror.

Daphne's lip curled. He was right—she didn't like what he was thinking.

"We need to see a psychic," Cayman blurted out anyway. And Daphne just groaned.

11.

"Help me, Daphne!" Maddy was covered in blood, her arms outstretched before her.

"Where are you, Maddy?"

"Only you can find me." Maddy ran up the hill like she'd done so many times before in Daphne's dreams. This time she left a trail of blood dripping from her body and guiding Daphne up the hill. "This way, Daphne. Hurry!"

Daphne followed, not even bothering to avoid the dry brush that littered the Southern California mountain. It crunched beneath her foot, sometimes scratching her leg. She didn't care. All that mattered was following the bloody little girl with the blonde pigtails.

The hill was getting steeper. They passed the tree

that Miguel and Daphne had been searching near just a few days before. Upward, higher and higher. Daphne's legs felt heavy beneath her, but Maddy continued gliding up the hill, seemingly weightless.

"Wait for me, Maddy. I'm trying to find you." Daphne could hear the desperation in her own voice.

"Find me, Daphne!" Maddy's voice echoed from somewhere on top of the hill, but Daphne could no longer see her. She had only the blood trail to guide her. It was getting heavier and thicker, like Maddy was losing more and more blood.

There was a tree with a low-lying branch in the path that Daphne barely registered because she was so focused on following the blood. She lifted the branch out of her face at the last second before it scratched her cheek.

And standing before her were both her parents. Beck Winters and Alanna Savage, two of the Hollywood elite, stood above a large pool of blood, staring ahead of themselves with unseeing eyes. They looked like zombies.

Maddy was nowhere.

"Look what you did, Daphne," they said in creepy unison.

"What?" Daphne whispered the question to her zombie parents. Nothing made sense. What were her parents doing here? What were they accusing her of? Where in the hell was Maddy?

"This is because of you, Daphne," they sang together again.

Afraid to look, but also drawn forward, Daphne inched up the hill to the pool of blood. Slowly, she allowed her eyes to look downward. Dread filled her stomach and made her nauseous.

The only thing she saw was her own reflection, shimmering in the blood as if it were now a pool of water with a red tinge.

Her own scream woke her up from the nightmare.

Daphne rubbed her face with her hands, wiping away the dream and the guilt. Her chest was heavy from the weight of it. Was she a victim or was she the perpetrator? Her subconscious kept sending her mixed signals.

"What happened, Daph?" Miguel was now sitting up next to her, his normally gelled-to-perfection hair disheveled from sleep.

Daphne paced in the moonlight, her mixed emotions driving energy throughout her body and making sleep impossible. "I'm connected somehow to Maddy's disappearance. I just know it."

"What makes you say that?"

"I don't even know how I know, but I just know. My dreams, my visions, my grandmother's spirit...they're all telling me the same thing." Daphne stopped pacing. She turned to stare at Miguel where he sat in a pool of moonlight streaming in from the motel window. "I'm involved somehow."

"You were just a child, Daphne. Whatever happened, I am positive you didn't have anything to do with Maddy Laurens' death and disappearance."

"But what if I did?" Daphne flopped on the foot of the bed. "What if I could have saved her years ago, but I didn't because I don't remember anything and I'm psychically blocked?"

Miguel scooted to the end of the bed and wrapped his good arm around her, pulling her in tight. She allowed herself to give in to his embrace, resting her head on his shoulder and letting her muscles loosen ever so slightly.

"Daphne, you have an amazing gift. You help people, both dead and alive, every single day." Miguel smoothed her short blonde hair as he spoke. "I know how frustrating it is to even let *one* bastard go. But you can't let that overshadow the hundreds of others you've stopped."

"Imagine you were a perfect shot with a firearm. That you could hit the bullseye every time in target practice," Daphne started to explain.

"I'm pretty good."

Daphne pulled back a little to face Miguel. "Now imagine that every time you went to shoot this one perpetrator, your firearm was jammed. That's how this case feels for me."

"So I guess we're awake now, huh?" Miguel smiled at Daphne. Sometimes he frightened her with how well he knew her. There was no way she could sleep now. There was too much going through her mind—and not enough details where the case of Maddy was concerned.

And maybe Miguel didn't understand the world of ghosts and psychics, but he did understand a case that eluded you.

"I always struggle to sleep after a Maddy Laurens nightmare," Daphne explained, as if she even needed to.

"I struggle to sleep when I am working through a case, too," Miguel answered, pulling her close again. "Maybe. Just maybe this psychic idea of Cayman's is a good idea. Perhaps she can sense what's blocking you."

Daphne sighed. The idea of another psychic studying her made her feel vulnerable in ways she hated to admit. Daphne liked to be the one in control. But they were at an impasse and they were running out of time. The thought of the LAPD taking the case back and cutting her out of it scared her far more than consulting another expert in her field. "I know."

"Six months ago, if someone told me I would not only believe in ghosts but also find myself in the presence of not one, but *two* psychics, I would have laughed in their faces." Miguel rested his chin on Daphne's head.

"People live in boxes. We all do, even me," Daphne responded. "When something doesn't fit in that box, we just flat out reject it. I guess it's too scary to realize how big the world actually is. And how small we actually are."

"Can I say something that might push your buttons?"

"If you actually dare," Daphne huffed.

"Your mom didn't seem so bad. Eccentric and melodramatic, but not awful. Why do you avoid her?" Miguel was truly curious. He had encountered far worse mothers in his line of work.

"I know what you're thinking." She did. "But it isn't as simple as her mothering skills. Alanna Savage is the poster child for everything I hated about that life. When you know, truly know, that there is a life after death, that your actions in this life *do* affect your afterlife, it just changes your perspective. I didn't want to play make-believe. I wanted to do real things." Daphne shifted so she could again face Miguel. "No one in Hollywood could understand that, believe me."

"You know what I think?" Miguel was smiling as he looked at Daphne there in the dark. Alanna Savage was beautiful, but not in the way Daphne was. Daphne's beauty was all-encompassing, her face, her mind, her soul. She just resonated completeness in a way that Miguel had never known. And it shined through even sitting here in the darkness. "I think you have an amazing perspective that you keep to yourself. Most of the time in everyday life, you respond with sarcasm and curt answers. But you never share your insightfulness."

Daphne made a face. "Most people aren't capable of facing the truth."

"Are you? Ready to face the truth?" Miguel grabbed her hand. He knew it would be hard for her.

She squeezed. As frightened as she sometimes was of their connection, she also craved it. He gave her a strength she'd never known she was missing all those years as a strong independent psychic woman. "Yes. I'm ready. Or at least, I'm ready to be ready."

Miguel leaned forward and kissed her forehead. It would be a few hours before it was even appropriate to be calling the other psychic.

But today would be the day they faced the truth about Daphne's past.

Miguel pulled her close and whispered to her hair, "I love you, Daphne Winters, psychic investigator."

Daphne drew in a deep breath. She hadn't said the words back to him yet, but there was no sense in denying it. They both knew the bond between them was bigger than love. Love was sacrifice, and there weren't very many people on this earth Daphne would make sacrifices for. But this man, who loved cleanliness and order, who was both tough and gentle, who could understand her in ways no one else ever could, this man she would lay down her life for.

"I love you, too." And this time, the truth of it gave her a sense of peace. And with the chaos of the Maddy Laurens case sending her every which way on the tempest, she clung to that safe harbor like it was the rock of Gibraltar.

12.

"Come on in." Cayman waved Miguel and Daphne into his home. "He'll be here in a few. And don't worry—I told him nothing. Just that we wanted a reading."

Daphne nodded. She had nothing to say. Obviously, she respected his profession as a fellow psychic medium, but being on the other side of the table was going to push her out of her normal comfort zone.

"Where were you thinking of doing the reading? In here?" Miguel gestured to the living room where they were all standing.

"Uh, yeah." Cayman looked around as he answered, as if to say he hadn't really had a plan about that. Yes, he'd watched Daphne work many a time, but it wasn't like he was an expert in these things. "Thanks for being open-minded, Daphne. I know it's a bit unusual."

"I was born open-minded." Daphne sat on the edge of the blue couch. The seat was warm from the mid-morning sun shining through the large front window. "But anyway, it's time to get some answers."

Cayman sat in an oversized chair next to where Daphne was sitting. "If I am being honest, I can't solve Maddy's case without you. There just isn't enough physical evidence. I'm as vested in this reading as you are."

Miguel sat right next to Daphne on the couch. He wasn't going to leave her side until she told him to. "But you're in control here, Daphne," he said. "If it gets to be too much, you just say the word."

Daphne shook her head. "I'm not afraid of my truth. Whatever it is, I plan to face it."

Miguel smiled. This girl was tough as nails.

"Hello?" a voice called from the screen door at Cayman's entryway.

Cayman pushed on his knees as he stood. "It's go time."

"I'm Mark Kang. Nice to meet you in person." Mark Kang extended a hand to Cayman as the screen door was opened. He was carrying a binder in his other hand.

"Winston Cayman." Cayman shook Mark's hand and then gestured to the living room where Miguel and Daphne were sitting. "This is Daphne and Miguel. We're focusing on Daphne today."

Daphne tried to smile at Mark in order to come across as an everyday lady, but it felt so foreign she was sure it looked forced. Instead, her mind was racing as she scanned the young psychic gentleman in front of her. He was unassuming, humble, and very calm. Daphne intuitively knew that he had had a wildly different upbringing than she had had. His family had always embraced and encouraged his gift.

Lucky bastard.

"Nice to meet you. I'm Mark." Mark smiled and it was full of warmth. The gentleness in his eyes instantly lowered everyone's blood pressure. The entire energy in the room was brought down several pegs, and Daphne knew it was no accident. This man could control the vibes. He was powerful. And she loved it.

"Let me explain my process." Mark unfolded the binder and spread it across his lap. From the pocket of the binder he pulled a ballpoint pen. "When I put pen to paper, it puts me in a bit of a trance, just to open me up to the area of my brain I need to do the reading. Sometimes I'll write words, but it also might just be scribbles. But don't worry, I never lose control of my consciousness."

Mark smiled at Daphne and she felt a calmness wash over her, almost to the point of being tired. Her limbs felt heavy and her eyelids droopy. Either this guy was really good, or her early morning wake-up call of a nightmare was hitting her suddenly.

"I understand," Daphne responded. She'd seen people use a similar method to Mark's before. Daphne preferred to become immersed in what she was sensing, but she knew some people preferred to channel it instead.

Mark continued looking at Daphne, even as he began drawing a large circle on the paper in front of him. Round and round he went with the pen, continuously scribbling out a circle. For the first time, his face changed. Contorted to something akin to a frown. "Sadness. No, that's not it. I sense loneliness. I feel someone who has felt like they were all alone in this world for a very long time. Independent and strong. Intense. Really tough. But spending a majority of their life in me-against-the-world mode."

Daphne nodded. She couldn't deny that he'd been describing her childhood and adolescence. In fact, until she met Duncan, she'd had no one in her life who understood her on any level.

"But there's something." Mark looked above Daphne, like the answer was floating above her head. "It's hard to describe. It's like a darkness. But a wall. Like a dark wall that's surrounding you."

Daphne shot up straight. He was sensing it too. A part of her had worried that she'd had some emotional blockage from a traumatic event, but if he was also sensing it as a wall, then it was more like the psychic block she'd been experiencing.

He stopped scribbling. "Are you also a sensitive?"

Daphne nodded slowly. She didn't want to lead this reading. She was trying to stay impassive, so she was hesitant to respond with words.

Mark pointed the pen at Daphne. "You're having trouble using your gift because of this wall." It wasn't a question. He knew. Daphne nodded again. It was comforting to have validation of her own belief.

"That's actually why you're here," Cayman explained. "We need to bring that wall down. How do we do that?"

Mark made eye contact with Daphne and she stared back at him. They wordlessly shared a meaning and understanding no one else in the room could partake in, because no one else in this room was psychic.

Only the two of them knew at this moment that this wasn't going to be a slam dunk.

"Only the person who put it there can bring it down," Mark stated.

Miguel stood up next to Daphne. He wasn't sure what Daphne was reacting to completely, but he fed off her response. And Daphne was overwhelmed by the realization that someone had been in her psyche. Someone had manipulated her. Someone had manipulated her gift. All along she'd been assuming it was some *thing*.

She'd never felt so violated.

"Who was it? Can you see?" Cayman asked. He either didn't care about Daphne's catharsis or he was just singularly focused on their case—or both.

"Daphne." Mark smiled as he said her name and she felt the emotions dissipate and her blood pressure lower again. She needed to ask him about how he did this. It was better than the most powerful drug. She slowly sat down and Miguel followed suit, sitting next to her. "Let's focus and see what we can uncover together."

Daphne nodded. Mark started scribbling again.

"Now, turn your intuition inward and focus on that barrier," Mark instructed. "You focus on that and I'll focus on you."

Daphne closed her eyes and breathed deeply. She opened up her senses and reached out, opening herself to the unseen world all around her. Miguel watched her closely, coiled and ready. Ready for what, he wasn't sure, but he sensed something was coming and it could be painful to Daphne.

Daphne continued digging, following her gift to the wall built around her memories. She saw flashes of her parents. Her childhood. Herself with pigtails. Herself with pigtails and covered with blood.

The pickaxe.

It was held by a male arm. "The tattoo!"

Maddy had tried to show her this tattoo many times but it had never come through. She could now see it clearly and she knew it was the arm that had killed Maddy. "It's a snake wrapped around a giant eyeball. On his forearm."

It was Cayman's turn to stand up. He knew the significance because Maddy had been trying to show Daphne for years. It was the one piece of evidence the young girl's spirit could share, but Daphne could never see it before.

"Maddy finally showed you the tattoo! This is huge." Cayman rubbed a hand across his thinning hair.

"I don't know who Maddy is," Mark replied, "but we're in Daphne's memories."

"What?" Miguel felt five steps behind everyone else.

Daphne just swallowed. Hard. She was linked now to Mark, so she knew what he knew. And his clarity was providing her a clarity she hadn't had with this case in a long time.

"This image wasn't put here by anyone. Daphne is remembering that tattoo and pickaxe from her own experiences. I can sense the young Daphne's absolute terror. You were very afraid of this man," Mark said.

Through her connection with Mark, she could

clearly see her memory for the first time. It was as if he could see through the wall in her psyche and because she was tethered to him, she could see through it for once also.

Her eight-year-old self grabbed the tattooed arm and pulled. She wasn't strong enough to overpower him even the slightest, but his surprise at her action forced him to let go of the pickaxe. It dropped from his hand and fell on her from above.

She was terrified. And in pain. The sharp sting from the wound on her face and shoulder hurting so much that Daphne was struggling to breathe just from simply witnessing the event. In her memory, a little girl's scream pierced the air. But it wasn't Daphne.

It was Maddy Laurens.

Daphne untethered from Mark, letting the connection close and slam shut. She covered her mouth in shock.

"It is all my fault. I was there. When Maddy died. It's my fault." Daphne couldn't process the details and the flood of emotions overwhelming her. Fear. Pain. Panic. Guilt. She ran out the front door of Cayman's home, holding her face where the pickaxe had sliced her in her memory.

"That can't be right," Miguel said to Mark as he sat dumbfounded.

Cayman leaned in. "What did you see?"

Mark shook his head. "She was struggling with the man with the tattoo and his pickaxe. I think she was fighting him off. Defending herself and another little girl."

"Another little girl?" Miguel asked, locking eyes with Cayman.

In response, Cayman pulled a photograph out of his pocket, the picture of Maddy he'd been carrying since they opened the file a few days before. "Was this the other little girl?"

Mark took only a half a glance at the photo Cayman was holding before confirming with a nod. "Yes, and..."

"And?" Cayman prodded.

"Her spirit is with us now. She's standing right beside you."

Cayman rubbed his arm from the chill he suddenly felt. He was used to Daphne talking to ghosts, but suddenly finding out one was standing right next to him was making his arm hairs stand straight.

"Daphne always said that Maddy's ghost only visited her in her dreams. And even when she did appear, she never spoke to Daphne." Miguel was trying to remember all the pieces of information about the ghost, hoping that one of them might be useful to the psychic now that Daphne was no longer in the room.

"Daphne was overcome by her survivor's guilt," Mark explained. "It's like an anchor on my chest, the way I feel it. But that's not what is blocking her memories. The man that hurt her did something to force her to forget."

"How is that even possible?" Miguel asked.

"Maddy? Do you know?" Mark asked the ghost in the room.

Miguel looked from the psychic to the empty

space next to Cayman where the psychic was looking. "Is she actually answering you?"

Mark stopped scribbling and looked at Miguel. "Yes. The man that injured Daphne and killed Maddy was able to block Daphne's abilities because he was also psychic."

"What?" Miguel felt his head swimming, he was so confused. "How can someone do that?"

Mark started packing up his belongings. "Similar to how Daphne and I were able to connect. He knew enough to get into her mind to stop her from sensing anything in his direction. When you stumbled on the Maddy Laurens case," Mark said, looking at Winston, "you stumbled right into the block that the killer had put there."

"So Daphne *is* a victim in this case, after all." Cayman rubbed his chin as he mulled over what they'd learned.

"And we have our biggest lead of all. Daphne was there, which means she and Maddy *were* connected somehow," Miguel added.

Mark stood, binder again tucked under his arm. "They were. A huge connection. In life, Maddy was also psychic."

13.

Daphne was sitting on the front porch crying when Mark Kang the psychic came marching out the front door. She quickly wiped away the tears. This was very much *not* something she wanted anyone to witness.

To her surprise, Mark sat down next to her.

Daphne looked away as if he would never know how she felt if she turned her head. *Yeah, right*. She knew better. He was probably drowning in her guilt as much as she was. He laid a hand gently on her back and she felt her emotions subside.

Damn, that was a good trick.

"You've spent your life trying to atone for that day," Mark said calmly. "But you have nothing to atone for. You did not kill Maddy Laurens."

"I could've stopped it from happening, but I was too weak," Daphne responded.

"No. You were a little kid." Mark stood up. "And there's still time to stop that snake-and-eyeball guy. You're getting close."

"You're leaving?" Daphne asked.

She knew philosophically he couldn't continue with their little adventure forever, but she had grown attached to him. Quite literally in a psychic sense. She didn't want him to go. It surprised her how much she'd actually enjoyed working with another psychic.

"You don't need me anymore." Mark started to walk toward his car. "You have her."

When Daphne looked up, Maddy Laurens stood before her.

"Who killed you, Maddy?" Daphne asked. It was a question to which she did not expect an answer. They had been here so many times before, and she would get flashes of a tree or a tattoo or something she couldn't hold onto, but never details.

But this time something was different.

"His name is Stryker. Or at least that's what everyone called him," Maddy answered.

"What?" It took Daphne a second to wrap her brain around the fact that Maddy was going to be able to help her. Had Mark broken down the walls?

"He made you forget, but it's all in your brain." Maddy was wearing a party dress and her hair was smooth. She looked ready for picture day. Daphne found it interesting that she chose to appear that way instead of how she died, as so many ghosts chose to do. But it was good. Her death was gruesome.

"Are you able to help me now?" Daphne asked.

"I've been with you all along. I just couldn't make you see," Maddy answered.

"Daphne?" Miguel opened the front door. "Who are you talking to?"

Cayman followed him out and they both stood next to where Daphne was sitting. Daphne gestured at the empty air, as if it were obvious. "Maddy."

"So she can communicate with you now? The block's gone?" Miguel asked, hopefulness seeping through in his voice.

"I think so. She told me the murderer was named Stryker." Daphne squinted up at Cayman.

"That's amazing!" Miguel was beaming, but when he looked between Cayman and Daphne, he didn't see them sharing his excitement. "Isn't it?"

"Do you remember that day yourself?" Cayman asked, his arms folded across his chest. It was obvious something wasn't sitting right with him.

"No." Daphne stood. "But I'm finally getting information from the victim herself. It's all we've ever wanted."

"You're still blocked." Cayman pointed at Daphne. "And you're a victim too."

"Come on, Winston." Miguel put his good hand on his hip. Sure, it would be nice to know exactly what happened to Daphne, but he didn't want to discount the breakthrough in the case they were actually working on.

"We find this asshole and we can make him undo whatever he did to Daphne."

"We need to figure this out carefully," Cayman said, speaking very closely. "This asshole, as you put it, is way ahead of us and he always will be."

Daphne sighed as the realization hit her. "He's psychic."

"That's how he found us," Maddy explained.

"Maddy, tell me what happened that day." Daphne pleaded for the answers that had been evading her for decades.

Cayman and Miguel watched Daphne, and Daphne watched Maddy. Only Daphne could hear the story but the men knew they'd be filled in, so they waited silently.

Maddy spoke to Daphne. "Stryker worked on your father's set for *Untold Angels*. Remember you and I would always play behind the trailers?" Daphne shook her head. She had no idea how it was possible, but she had no memory whatsoever of playing with Maddy on her father's set. Maddy continued, "Well, my dad also worked on the set as part of the crew, so we actually did spend a lot of time together. We all knew Stryker and liked him. I remember my dad saying he was a hard worker and a friendly guy. I guess he had us all snowed."

"How was he able to fool you and me? We're psychic too," Daphne asked.

Maddy's ghost shrugged. "We were kids. He was able to overpower us psychically too. But he won everyone's trust. So when I saw him walking home from school that day, I wasn't scared at all."

"How did he get you inside the abandoned house on the corner?" Daphne asked. Maddy had no reason to lie anymore and she said she'd trusted Stryker. But to follow him into a strange house just wasn't sitting right with Daphne, even if they were only eight.

But Maddy shook her head. "He staged that crime scene with my blood after the fact. He took me to the mountains. You were already there so, again, I had no reason to fear for my life."

"I was in the mountains?" The blood drained from

Daphne's face. She knew she was there that day from the fragmented memory Mark had unlocked, but she'd been kidnapped too? Her blocked memories were really starting to drive her crazy. How could she forget being kidnapped?

Maddy placed a gentle hand on Daphne's. She felt a soft pressure from the spirit's energy. "There's more, Daphne."

"I was kidnapped, seriously injured, and you died. And there's *more*?" Daphne was feeling overwhelmed, but that continued frustration with her own memories and psychic intuition not coming through was the worst feeling of all. It felt like being a tennis player who suddenly lost use of their arms and had to learn to play without them.

Maddy nodded. "You weren't kidnapped. Your dad was there too."

"Beck Winters was an accessory to murder?" Daphne asked Maddy, but looked at Miguel and Cayman, clueing them in to details she was learning and they couldn't hear.

"What?" Miguel couldn't hide his shock. Daphne was in way deeper than any of them had suspected.

"He wasn't there for the murder, but he knew Stryker was a psychic and was 'testing things' as he put it, on our minds," Maddy explained.

"My dad knew. My dad knew so much." Daphne was shaking her head as if this very act could make the puzzle pieces fit.   She'd always had a hard time understanding her dad. And his vapid life choices had made it very difficult to respect him. But now? Now she felt like she could be free with her feelings of hatred.

She hated her father right now.

"You need to fill us in." Miguel couldn't hide his anxiety. Hearing only one side of the story and waiting patiently for the rest was wearing down his calm demeanor.

"Stryker was doing experiments on me and Maddy. And my dad was there. He may not have hurt us, but he was complicit," Daphne explained.

"Are you remembering anything on your own

yet?" Cayman asked again. When Daphne shook her head, he added, "Maybe you should tether yourself to Maddy like Mark did with you, so you can at least see her memories?"

Daphne hesitated. Not because she didn't want to know the truth, but because this was all too personal. Other cases she'd worked on happened to *other people*. Up until Maddy's death, she and Maddy had been friends. And victims.

And somehow Daphne escaped with her life and that only served to make her more guilty. Was Mark Kang right and her whole career had been so important to her simply because she'd escaped Maddy's fate?

Daphne fought the overwhelming feeling of nausea that was coming over her.

"Okay, that's enough. Daphne needs a break." Miguel pulled her close to his chest.

Cayman shook his head. "Not until we find Stryker. We can't do this without her and we have hours left before we hand over the case."

"You and I can interview Beck Winters. All we need is Stryker's last name. Maybe even a real first name. And to know how much Beck Winters actually knew," Miguel argued.

"That will all be hearsay. Daphne can give us a firsthand account as soon as she can remember," Cayman pushed back.

Daphne shoved Miguel off and waved her arms at both gentlemen. "Stop! I never said I wouldn't do it." She turned to Miguel. "My dad always cared about his career more than he did about me. I haven't seen him in years and after learning how involved he was, I definitely don't want to approach that man unless it's with an arrest warrant." She turned to Maddy. "Show me everything, Maddy."

Wordlessly, Maddy reached out a pale, ghostly arm to Daphne, and Daphne reached back until their fingers touched. The connection was instant. Daphne felt like she was traveling rapidly down a dark tunnel where visions and memories appeared for an instant on the dark walls.

And then she was there.

It was a small room made entirely of wood. Wood floors, wood walls, wooden beams across the ceiling. The head of a stag was mounted majestically above a large fireplace.   Furniture was mismatched and covered in brightly colored, crocheted throws.

It looked like an old lady's cabin.

A big man with muscular arms stood above two girls who sat obediently on the couch. Daphne noticed the snake and eyeball tattoo. *Stryker*. He was explaining to them why they were there.

"You two are special, like me. We can do things other people can't do. Did you know that?" He was speaking softly in a hushed, low tone, but it lacked the tenderness that most people used when speaking to children. Through adult eyes, Daphne was able to see he was a monster. The two innocent young girls nodded their heads dutifully in response to his question.

"So, we're going to play a little game," Stryker

explained as he began pacing. "We're going to see who can get inside the other person's head and get them to do things. Like stand on one leg. You order me with my mind and see if you can make me do it. Doesn't that sound fun?"

The blank look on the young faces told Daphne all she needed to know. They were skeptical that this was an exercise in fun. But they had no reason to be afraid. Stryker was their friend, wasn't he?

When you're eight, your brain doesn't go to dark places like murder. You just think to yourself that this game doesn't sound very fun. But neither girl wanted to be rude and say that out loud.

"Do you want me to go first?" Stryker grinned and his façade of being a "friend" completely shattered and fell away in a thousand pieces. The girls squirmed for the first time.

Adult Daphne thought to herself, *where the hell is my dad*?

Daphne had never understood her father or felt close with him, but today's realizations were making her hate him. He abandoned her to this creep. And even if he wasn't a complete lunatic, common sense would tell you that you shouldn't leave two little girls in the company of a strange man.

But wherever he was, Beck Winters wasn't here when Stryker started his experiments.

Stryker locked eyes with Daphne. *So I was first,* Daphne again realized as an adult. The man began to squint and it was clear he was concentrating. Like a powerful jolt, the memory slammed into Daphne's mind—not what she was watching, but what she *remembered.*

The pickaxe.

She remembered seeing it in the cabin and thinking at the time that it was out of place. But then she remembered being overwhelmed with the desire to pick it up. A feeling like being drugged almost. She felt loopy with heavy limbs. And she had energy for nothing else except getting the pickaxe.

Eight-year-old Daphne complied.

She walked over to where the weapon sat on an

ugly wooden table. Adult Daphne begged the little girl not to do what she knew she'd already done. She reached out and gripped the cold, metal handle. It was heavy for a small child, and she spent a moment feeling its weight. Swaying the small device back and forth as if she were using a machete.

It was clear that Stryker had somehow gotten in her mind and compelled her. That was violating enough, but Daphne was breathing heavily over the real question. *What exactly did he want me to do with it?* And what scared her even more was that Daphne didn't know.

She was looking back on a situation where, despite her ability, she was completely vulnerable. He could make her do anything.

"Very good." Stryker flashed a venomous smile. As soon as he spoke the words, the drugged feeling dissipated and Daphne quickly dropped the pickaxe. He then turned to Maddy. "Your turn."

Maddy swallowed hard but said nothing. She had fear in her eyes, but not as much as Daphne felt she should. She still trusted this bastard. And why shouldn't she? Nothing really bad had happened. Yet.

Daphne watched as Maddy became droopy-eyed and then followed Daphne over to the wooden table. Only she reached beyond where the pickaxe had been and grabbed a candlestick. Similar to Daphne, she took a moment to feel it cold and heavy in her hands before placing it back where it had been.

And then suddenly the image was gone, and Daphne was snapped back to present day and standing on Cayman's porch.

"Wait. What happened next?" Daphne was frantic.

"That was the first time he experimented on us," Maddy stated. Weirdly, she looked much older than the eight her ghost portrayed, as if her wisdom continued to grow even if her body never did. Her spirit was wary. And it all served to frustrate Daphne the more.

"What do you mean, the first time?" Daphne wanted to explode from the pent-up emotions.

"What did you see?" Miguel ran to Daphne's side, his own desire to understand the missing puzzle pieces driving him. Somehow Cayman knew to stand back and wait his turn. He just watched everything unfold.

Daphne waved Miguel off. "He practiced mind control on us. Apparently, several times." She turned back to Maddy. "You've got to give me something."

"Can I show you where to find me now? I think you'll find the answers you need there." Maddy's voice was soft. Defeated. Ready for eternal rest.

Daphne nodded.

After twenty-seven years, it was time to end this. Daphne was ready. For answers. For closure. For confrontation. She wasn't going to rest until there was justice for Madison Laurens.

14.

They were back in the Santa Monica Mountains. The sun was filling the sky and overwhelming the landscape with its heat. There wasn't a cloud to be seen for miles, nothing to slow down the sun from its constant attack of rays. Daphne wiped her forehead with the back of her hand, wishing desperately she had thought to bring a water bottle.

But the heat wasn't the only reason she was sweating.

She had been here so many times before. Lost, frustrated, heading nowhere. But this time she *knew* she was going to find Maddy. After all these years. After countless nightmares of chasing Maddy's ghost. After coming to these mountains again and again and staring blankly at nothing.

This time Maddy's ghost was really leading her. Both she and Maddy had a determination and—thanks to Mark Kang—a connection that Daphne had never before thought possible.

Cayman and Miguel had been trying to follow dutifully with very few questions. The restraint was not easy. Miguel was finding that not seeing and hearing Maddy was just as difficult for him as it must've been for Daphne all these years. He wasn't used to trusting blindly.

But he also knew Daphne was in the zone and she would explain when she could. She always had. Miguel knew this Daphne. She was a bloodhound on the scent and if he broke her tracking with a slew of questions, it would enrage her. Or worse yet, she would lose the scent. He had no way of knowing how precarious her sudden ability to hear Maddy truly was. Was it cured? Or was it temporary? Whatever the situation, he wasn't going to risk jeopardizing anything. It wasn't his case, but it was important to Daphne, so it was important to him.

"This way," Maddy said over her shoulder. Daphne had to shake her head to get rid of the memory of her nightmares. Maddy had led her deep in mountains to nowhere before countless times in her dreams, and even though she was wide awake, it was difficult to erase those previous letdowns. "Only you can find me, Daphne."

Just as she had in so many dreams before, Daphne followed Maddy's coaxing up the hill, between trees, over shrubs. The feeling was surreal, like déjà vu. Every step, every sight, every sound was familiar and yet more real this time. This time they were going to go somewhere. This time would be different. Just like in her dream, Maddy disappeared behind a tree and Daphne momentarily panicked. Would she see Maddy on the other side? She stepped forward and was pummeled by the sound of her parents' voices.

"This is all your fault, Daphne!"

Daphne stopped and looked around. This wasn't a dream. She was hearing their voices chorusing just like she did in her sleep last night.

Maddy poked her head around the tree and the sight of her gave Daphne relief.

"Daphne? You okay?" Miguel immediately had a hand on the small of her back. She appreciated the gesture. She didn't know what to make of everything that came at her with this case, but it was refreshing to not be alone this time. She had Miguel. And Maddy. And Cayman.

It may not be the family she was born into, but Daphne had learned that family was often what you made it. Family was there when you needed them. Family was made up of the people who believed in you no matter what craziness ensued. Birth was happenstance, but it didn't magically create bonds and support systems. After a childhood of neglect, mistrust, even dislike, Daphne had forged a new family. A family based on faith, support, and determination.

No matter what lay on the trail ahead, whatever part her parents played, Daphne knew she could face this. Because she had these people by her side.

She sucked in a large breath. "I'm fine." She grabbed Miguel's good hand from behind her back and squeezed. "Maddy, take me all the way this time."

"We're almost there." The little ghost girl with the pigtails turned and started back up the mountain. Daphne recognized the tree she and Miguel had been hovering near just a few days ago. But Maddy continued upward. *So I was wrong about the tree.* Not too surprising since she'd had a psychic blindfold on all these years thanks to Stryker.

When it felt like they would surely turn to liquid from prolonged exposure to the sun's rays, Maddy turned and ventured off the hiking trail. Daphne took a moment to inspect where they were. She could see the Valley laid out before her. In fact, the view was stunning. They were about three-quarters of the way to the top and there was no one else around. Hiking trails were popular in these mountains, but not in the peak heat of the day. Or at night. Stryker would have had plenty of time to hide Maddy's remains with no one watching.

The brush was thicker and dryer off the trail and the sharp branches grabbed at Daphne's skirt, as if they were warning her to stop and turn back. As if the very mountain itself were telling her things were only going to get worse from here.

There was a large boulder resting against the side of a hill. The kind that would annihilate everything beneath it if an earthquake knocked it loose. It stood like a statue in front of a shrine. So it was fitting when Maddy stopped right in front of it.

"Here." Maddy touched the rock. "I'm behind here."

"Here," Daphne whispered as she copied Maddy's movements, gently touching the boulder. As soon as she did, images flashed in her mind. A garbled mix of video clips. A little girl running from a man with a snake-and-eyeball tattoo. A pickaxe coming down again and again. The background mountains, trees, dry brush and boulders. A little girl's remains tossed aside behind a boulder like she was the trash. Daphne's parents.

Choosing to ignore the last image, Daphne turned to Cayman. "She's buried here. Can we get a crew out right now?"

Cayman nodded. "I'll call Derek." After all these years, they couldn't wait another second. The Laurens family would finally have their closure.

"Are we going to be cited? Since the case is now officially open with the LAPD?" Miguel asked Cayman.

Cayman sighed, placing his hands on his hips. "Nah. As it turns out, Derek was the one that got the case re-opened. Weird little twist of events, huh?"

"Oh," was all Miguel could think of to say. Daphne ignored them both. She only wanted answers about Maddy right now. The who's-case-is-it-anyway pissing contest could wait as far as she was concerned.

Daphne turned to Maddy. "How did he get your DNA all over the abandoned house?"

Maddy shook her head. She looked tired again, as if she couldn't wait another moment for this to end so she could go to her eternal rest. "He did everything right here.

Cut my body into pieces and took what he needed. To fake out the cops."

It had been an effective maneuver. It had worked on the cops and on Daphne herself for decades. But, of course, as a psychic, he probably knew that would happen.

"She died out here?" Cayman asked, filling in gaps that he couldn't hear but presumed from Daphne's line of questioning.

"Yeah. The abandoned house was a head fake."

"Damn." It was all Cayman could think of to say.

"Can you also ask Derek to start hunting down Stryker? He worked in Hollywood and he has a distinct tattoo. We have to be able to find this guy."

"One step ahead of you, little lady. I texted him when we were still back at the house and you were having your weird memory-lane vacation with our vic." Cayman winked at Daphne. She just rolled her eyes in response.

"Daph. Do you feel anything here?" Miguel asked. Always Daphne. His concern was singularly focused on her.

And a part of Daphne was hesitant to open up. But she also knew she had to try.

Daphne knelt on the ground and laid her palms on the dirt behind the large boulder. And she opened her mind, releasing the piece of her psyche that connected freely with the world around her. She saw a flash of a little girl running. This one was Daphne as a small child. She was running and looking over her shoulder.

This little girl knew Stryker was bad.

Then the image changed and it was Maddy running and looking over her shoulder. She was in these hills. After being kidnapped a block from her own home by someone her family trusted, she'd been tied up and beaten on top of having her mind manipulated. Then she was let loose so she could be controlled one last time— and hunted. She was running scared, even though she couldn't resist the instructions that were forced into her brain.

"Keep looking. It's just behind this rock." Daphne heard Stryker's slimy voice instructing Maddy. Using his psychic ability to convince her there was a present for her hidden in the mountains. What a piece of shit.

And then he pulled out a gun. While her back was to him and she looked for her present, he shot her in the back. What a coward.

"It wasn't a pickaxe. He shot her." Daphne shook her head. Her emotions were overtaking her again. Frustration. Anger. The need for justice. "He's been tricking me since the start." She kept reaching, opening her mind further and further.

Where are you, you bastard?

She saw a family in mourning. A movie set crew stricken with grief and shock that one of their own could go missing. Stryker hiding out in his cabin. Daphne knew so much had happened at that cabin. They needed to find it. And, like so many times in her life, clarity formed in her mind. On any case but this one, it would have been just another day at the office. But today, with this case, it was a miracle.

She *knew* where the cabin was. Just down the

road, on a street with only dirt and pebbles, a black mailbox announced its presence. You would drive by if you weren't looking for it. Daphne was looking. Reaching. Striving.

"Hello, Daphne." The slimy voice was suddenly in her head. And this was real time, not in the past. "Long time, no see. And the truth is, I've missed you."

Daphne recoiled at the sound of the monster's voice, but she didn't want to lose the connection. He was in her head—but she was in his too. *Gotcha, you rat bastard.*

"Hi, Stryker. I'd say it's a pleasure, but you actually make me want to barf." Daphne was talking to her psychic connection with the killer, but the words were spoken out loud. Miguel knelt down beside her in the dirt, not knowing what to do to protect her but feeling this was too much for her to be doing alone. Connecting psychically with a psychopath felt really dangerous.

"I've been watching you. Popping in from time to time. Fresno, huh?" Stryker was trying to intimidate her, distract her. And even though her heart was pounding at the very sound of his voice and knowing he'd been able to spy on her all these years, she wasn't an innocent eight-year-old anymore.

"Yeah, you're a real macho man, using mind tricks to hide away like a little bitch." Two can play at this game. Daphne decided to chat with him while she pinpointed his location. She was finding this murderer. Today.

This all ends today.

Her words made him laugh. The sound of his laughter made her want to punch something. When she was eight, she ran from this man. But after all these years, she was tired, frustrated and angry. Fueled by the need to right the wrong done to Maddy, her childhood friend that she hadn't even remembered. Because he'd taken that away from her too. She was psychically running toward him now. And she was going to find him.

He'd had the upper hand as a grown man playing games with two little girls. But those days were so far in the past there was a layer of dust all over them. Daphne raised a hand toward the cabin. He wasn't there. She knew that. But where the hell was he?

"Daphne, Daphne, Daddy's little girl. Looks like you never forgave him and you didn't even really know why until now." He was laughing at her again. She wanted to rip his tattooed arm off his body and shove it down his throat.

But he was also right, and that was the part that angered Daphne the most. She still wasn't exactly sure what role her father had played in all this. But she wasn't going to admit that openly. "It's over, Stryker. You can't control me anymore."

"I've been doing it for years, sweets." Ugh, his voice made her retch. "You don't even know what I did to you."

He was right again, but Daphne couldn't process that. She stayed focused on finding him. Her arms were acting like antennae as she reached out through time and space to grab his location. Keep him talking, keep him talking. "That's where your narcissism is showing, asshole.

I don't care what you did to me. I care what you did to Maddy." Mostly true.

"But we had so much fun. I promise you, you enjoyed our time together. Playing with weapons." Styker sighed. Daphne kept searching. "Maddy had to die. She was a liability. I hated to do it, but she never played along. You, though." She felt him sneering. "You were a willing participant. You loved the mind games, Daphne. You might have been a little girl, but you were twisted."

That truth bomb hurt a bit, but Daphne chose to push past it. She was close. She could feel it. She was getting close to him. *Keep him talking*. "You're trying to say I was a psycho like you?"

He laughed again. "That's exactly what I'm saying. You paint me as the bad guy. But you and I? We're very much the same."

She wanted to scream at him. She wanted to slap him as she yelled how different they were, but she couldn't. She was so close to finding him. "So I was able to use mind control?"

"You were a complete natural."

She'd been making conversation, but the realization of what he was saying stopped her in her tracks. He laughed again and it knocked her out of her stupor. She could spend time on what he was saying later.

Right now, she'd found him. She locked in on his location and then said, "Oh yeah? Well, I've always been a badass."

"And that's why you're still alive." Oh, he made her flesh feel like it was covered in bugs.

But she didn't care anymore. She had his location and as was so often the case with her psychic ability, she suddenly knew without a doubt how to turn off this connection. "Hope you've enjoyed our little reunion. Because the game's over now, Stryker."

And she slammed their connection closed before he could utter another thought in her direction.

As she opened her eyes and came back psychically to the mountain by Maddy's body, Miguel helped her stand. "What? What happened? Were you talking to the murderer?"

"I know where he is. But we have to hurry. Everything I know about him, he also knows about me," Daphne explained to Miguel.

"Derek's on his way with a team," Cayman said. "Why don't you give them a minute and a blue can go with you?"

Daphne shook her head. "No time. He's probably packing at this very moment." She started walking to the trail that led back to the car.

"Daphne, he's a murderer. You can't just appear in front of him and think this is going to go smooth." Miguel was pleading with her. He still had one arm in a sling and a psychic murderer was an adversary that needed to be handled with full strength.

Daphne smiled. It felt so freeing to finally be able to see this case as clearly as she should've all these years. Stryker couldn't control her anymore. "If Stryker could have, he would have killed me when I was eight. He cleared my memory because that was *all* he could do. He can't control me." And she knew with complete certainty that these words were true.

The vision popped in her head as the words came from her mouth. Once he had controlled her with the pickaxe that first time, she had learned. He had unwittingly trained her on how to get others to do what you wanted. And then she also knew how to block him. After that, all he could do was erase Daphne's memory and play with Maddy until she was more of a liability than an asset. Deep in her wiped subconscious Daphne had remembered she was loosely related to Maddy and Stryker, so she'd carried the guilt all the years after—but nothing else.

But how had she cut her face with the pickaxe? And how was her father involved? She'd have to tackle these questions, but first she had to stop Stryker before he ran.

"Cayman, can we take your car and you have a patrol officer follow us?" Miguel asked. He knew he had to support Daphne—nothing would stop her anyway—but he also had to keep her safe. Sometimes it was exhausting following Daphne headfirst into confrontations with violent offenders.

He was never more frustrated not to have two good arms.

"Good idea," Cayman nodded. "What's the address, Daphne?"

The look she gave him was filled with pity. She felt sorry for such ignorance. "I don't know the address. I just *know* where it is. I'll turn when my intuition tells me."

Cayman stared at her. "Well, that's not going to make this easy. What do I tell the officer? Go where Daphne's intuition leads you?"

"Yes," answered Daphne.

Miguel took a deep breath. "Just give them your license plate number and tell them to head to the base of the mountain. Anyone nearby will be able to catch up." He put a hand at Daphne's elbow. "Let's go. Before Stryker bolts."

They began running down the mountain, but

Cayman stopped them when he called out, "Daphne!" She turned and he tossed her his keys. "Get that bastard."

She nodded. "That's the plan."

"We'll call you when he's apprehended. Let us know when the team finds Maddy's remains," Miguel said to Cayman, and then he and Daphne continued down the mountain as fast as they could go, Daphne holding Miguel's hand in case he slipped with only one good arm to catch himself.

"Maybe this wasn't the best activity for your recovery," Daphne said.

"Nonsense. I've never felt better." Miguel smiled at her. In a way, it wasn't totally untrue. If he wasn't constantly worried about Daphne, he'd be enjoying the thrill of the hunt. He lived for catching the bad guy—and what could be a worse "bad guy" than a grown man manipulating, abusing and then murdering innocent young girls? Injury or no injury, he would relish stopping this guy.

"I have to be honest with you." Daphne spoke the words slowly despite their hustle down the mountain trail.

Opening up wasn't something she was used to, but it was different with Miguel. Being honest with him felt like being honest with herself. "Stryker is just as much connected to me as I am to him. I know how to block him now, but still…he knows my thoughts and feelings." She stopped so she could look Miguel in the eyes, make sure he understood. "He'll know you're important to me and he'll use that against me."

Miguel took a strand of Daphne's short hair and smoothed it out. Her signature disheveled hair style was cute, but it felt like the right thing to do to prep her for her oncoming confrontation. Miguel liked things tidy. "We'll face this like we will face everything in life. Together. Our souls are linked, right?"

Daphne smiled. He would stay by her side just as she'd stay by his. There was no avoiding it. She wagged a finger at him and then continued down the hill. "You didn't even believe in soul mates until you met me."

"I didn't believe in a lot of things until I met you."

Cayman's car was just up ahead and the sight of it

gave them the fuel to pick up their speed. They climbed in and Daphne turned the engine. Normally she would close her eyes to feel where they were going, but with Miguel's arm in a sling it would be much easier for her to drive, and so she'd need to do this with her eyes open.

Head south.

She started driving at double the speed limit. *Let the cops try to pull me over—at least then they'll be with me when I pull up next to a child killer.* The tires on Cayman's car spewed dust every which way as Daphne raced at top speed into the Valley.

They hadn't gone very far when Daphne sensed she'd need to turn right. Red light or no, traffic or clear, she turned right without slowing down. The tires screeched their objections to her reckless driving. Daphne sped up all the more.

The streets were lined with small time shops: vacuum repair companies, laundromats, stationary stores. They all whizzed by as Daphne floored it.

Left turn.

The sound of other cars squealing as they slammed on their brakes to avoid hitting Cayman's car echoed through the Valley. Miguel grabbed the handle above the passenger door and held tight.

Daphne noticed a patrol car following her in the rearview mirror, but their lights weren't flashing. "I wonder if that's who Cayman called."

Miguel turned around and saw the car with two uniformed police officers racing through the streets right behind Cayman's car. He exhaled in utter relief. "Looks like it. If not, they'd be arresting you right now. I never knew you could drive like a race car driver."

Right turn. Cars veered every which way as Daphne, and then the police car, turned right. After that intersection they turned their lights and siren on. Daphne pushed the accelerator all the more, assuming they were a police escort and not trying to pull her over. It was a gamble, but she was willing to take it.

Another right turn. This time onto a tree-lined street that curved up a small hill. The houses weren't elaborate but they were nice, well-kept. Very middle-class suburban.

Miguel prayed there weren't any children playing in the streets as Daphne plowed through far faster than she should in a residential neighborhood.

Daphne's eyes narrowed. "I've got you, ass hat." And she pushed the accelerator even harder. Miguel followed her line of sight and saw only a black sedan with tinted windows.

"Is that him?"

Daphne nodded. "Sorry, Cayman."

And she sped up, as fast as the car could go. Faster than Miguel had ever gone on a residential street. And then the front of Cayman's car collided with the black sedan, pushing the sedan several feet in front of them and both cars screeching to a halt, metal crunching and glass shattering upon impact.

15.

It took Miguel and Daphne a moment or two to get their bearings after the accident. Damn if Miguel's shoulder wasn't throbbing like this had been a very bad idea for his recovering gunshot wound.

Her head spinning, Daphne unfastened her seat belt and climbed out of Cayman's car. Slowly, Miguel followed her as the patrol car parked behind them, lights still flashing.

"Where'd he go?" Daphne asked when she'd opened the driver's side door. "Dammit."

"He can't have gotten far." Miguel looked every which way, but the neighborhood seemed peaceful, serene.

Daphne stopped and looked at the white house in front of them. "I know where he is." She stepped forward, but Miguel caught her arm and pulled her back.

"Daph, let the police arrest him. You've done your job. Let them do theirs."

He was right. Of course, he was right. What was Daphne going to do? Wrestle this murderer to the ground? So Daphne turned and walked over to the police officers who were climbing out of their car.

"We were told to follow you. Luckily your maniac driving made you easy to spot. Care to fill us in on what's going on?" The taller of the two gentlemen was speaking. His name tag said "Price."

"There's a murderer hiding out in those bushes. He's wanted for the cold case murder of Madison Laurens. Go arrest him." Daphne pointed to where she knew Stryker was hiding.

Officer Price just raised an eyebrow. It was clear he thought she was completely insane.

Miguel flashed his badge. "Detective Alvarez, Fresno P.D. She's telling the truth. We've been working with Detective Cayman to catch this guy. He's possibly armed and definitely dangerous."

Officer Price took Miguel much more seriously, although skepticism still lined his brow. But he nodded at his fellow officer and then casually strolled to the bushes. After speeding through the San Fernando Valley at reckless speeds and almost killing herself and Miguel in the car crash that stopped this bastard from escaping, Daphne did not very much enjoy their cavalier attitudes.

"A little pep in your step wouldn't hurt you," Daphne shouted at the two officers.

"Daphne," Miguel muttered. But the officers ignored her anyway. They walked over to the bushes and glanced in the flowerbeds. Then they looked back at Daphne with a frown.

"Anywhere else he could've gone? There's no one here," Officer Price stated, his voice laced with pity at the deranged woman he was told to follow.

"No. Daphne is never wrong." Miguel marched over to the bushes and looked for himself. "Hmmm. They're right. He's not here anymore, Daph."

Dammit. Mind control.

They weren't used to an adversary like this one. This was superhero comic book type stuff. It was clear she was on her own with this guy.

"If you're a real man, you'll at least face me, you coward," she called toward the hedges where she *knew* Stryker was still hiding.

"You mean *us*." Maddy appeared next to Daphne.

With the devil's grin on his thin, pasty lips, Stryker stood. "The whole gang's back together again. But who's the broad?" He gestured with his chin to the right of Daphne.

Daphne looked and then confirmed, "This is Grandma Jean."

Miguel ran over to Daphne. "Are you talking to Stryker? Where is he? Why can't I see him?"

"If there's nothing here for us, we're going to leave," Officer Price said as he and his partner started back toward their patrol car.

"No, no, no," Miguel pleaded. "This is far from

over. Give her a moment. Please. She's a psychic and so is the murderer." The officers looked like they were dealing with crackheads, but thankfully they didn't leave.

"So, your little boyfriend knows all about me, huh?" Stryker sneered.

"This is between us girls," Daphne responded. Whatever happened, he couldn't leave this suburban home's front yard.

"You should probably know, my sweet Daphne" Stryker started casually moving toward his car. "I've only gotten more powerful over the years."

Don't let him leave. "Oh yeah? Well, so have I. Little girls are easy prey, but a woman and two ghosts? Not so much."

And with that, the ghost of Maddy Laurens rushed to meet Stryker where he stood. Despite her tiny stature, she was able to prevent him from continuing his stroll. He laughed it off, but his ego was bruised.

"I wanted to simply move on and leave all this behind me." Stryker reached in his pocket and pulled out a pocketknife. "But you're not going to let me, are you?"

Daphne folded her arms across her chest. "You're a real mind reader. And if you think you're getting anywhere near me with that knife, you're really losing your touch."

He stared intensely at Daphne. No words passed between them as he studied her and she studied him. Both powerful adversaries. Neither going to yield.

"It isn't for you," Stryker smiled.

Daphne opened her mind to discover his true intent, but instead of clarity her mind got foggy. Her limbs became heavy. Slowly, she stepped forward with big clunky steps. One step, two step, three...four.

"Daphne, no!" Grandma Jean cried out. "Fight this."

Fight what? Daphne continued clunking to Stryker, reaching a hand toward his sadistically smiling face.

"Good girl. I knew you were still a willing pupil." Stryker went to hand the knife to Daphne, but Maddy hit it and it went flying.

"Whoa! Where'd that come from?" Officer Price reacted to seeing the knife seemingly fly out of nowhere.

But Miguel, rightfully, knew enough to know that things weren't right. He ran to Daphne's side. "What's he doing to you, Daph?"

She stared at Miguel, seeing right through him. All she could think about was getting that knife. She pushed past him and followed the knife. Stryker watched the whole thing with superb satisfaction. A few more clunky steps and the knife was at her feet. She bent down and picked it up, feeling the weight of it in her hands—just like the pickaxe all those years ago. The metal was cold and firm. It felt good. It felt *right*.

Shling. She popped open the switchblade.

"Perfect, Daphne," Stryker sneered. With a nod toward Miguel, he commanded, "Now kill him."

Daphne stared at the knife in her hand. *Yes, kill him*. She clunked a heavy foot forward in a big robotic step.

And then Maddy's ghost and Grandma Jean were standing in front of her, blocking her path. Maddy put a small hand out, stopping Daphne's advance.

"You're stronger than this, Daphne," Grandma Jean stated. "You were stronger than Stryker at eight-years-old. You're much stronger than he is now. This is *your* power. *Your* psyche. It's time to end this."

"Yeah, Grandma Jean," Stryker laughed. "She's so strong she was about to murder her boyfriend. *Because I told her to.*"

"Daphne?   What's going on?" Miguel asked, watching Daphne stand there staring at him with a knife in her hand. He knew she would never hurt him, but his frustration was building. He might not be psychic, but he knew enough to know something was very wrong.

Daphne stared at the knife in her hand and then looked back at Miguel. She knew she was supposed to kill him but she couldn't figure out why. Her brain was so foggy.

"Daphne."   She heard Maddy's voice from far

away. *Yes, Maddy. I'm helping Maddy. By killing Miguel?*

"Daphne. Push him out. Stryker is in your brain."

And like a switch was flipped, Daphne realized Maddy's words were true. He was in her brain. Oh, hell no! She pushed back on the haze and it lifted from her brain, like a mist dissipating as the sun comes out. She dropped the knife in her hand as if it were on fire and she took a step back from Stryker.

"What?" he asked with a shrug.

"Daphne, are you okay?" Miguel asked, keeping an arm out toward Officer Price, who stood at the ready as he watched this crazy lady in a Bohemian skirt wield a pocketknife in broad daylight on this quiet, residential street.

"He got in my head," Daphne said, shame lacing her words.

Stryker just stood there, smiling, zero fear. Only Daphne among the living could even see him, and he had just proven he could still control her. Everything was going his way.

"Where do we go from here, Daphne?" Stryker asked, as if they were at an impasse.

"Daphne, make him show himself to the police. We just need him to pay for his crimes," Maddy pleaded. Her soul wanted rest. *Needed* it, really.

Daphne shook her head, rattled by the fact he'd been so easily able to control her. She'd thought she'd be stronger now after all this time. "His gift is too powerful."

Grandma Jean put a gentle hand on Daphne's shoulder. "That's the eight-year-old version of you talking. And it's flat out not true. Do you know why Stryker weaseled his way onto your father's set? And why he singled you out? Because this was *your* gift. And he wanted it."

Daphne was just about to push back on her grandmother for again stating things that made no sense. Mind control was something *she* taught *Stryker*? But when he turned and started running up the street, she knew it must be true.

It's all about you, Daphne. It always has been.

Shit.

Daphne sighed when she realized what she had to do. She really didn't relish the thought.

She was going to have to get inside the head of a sadistic, child-killing, manipulative asshole.

16.

Nothing had ever disgusted Daphne more.

In her lifetime and profession, she had done some uncomfortable things. There were dark secrets revealed. There were dark spirits to battle. Hell, she'd even taken on a demon. But pushing her way into the mind of a child-murderer was setting the bar to a new and agonizing height.

And this was the child-murderer who had toyed with her mind and blocked out pieces of her childhood, robbing her of memories from a pivotal time in her life. He wasn't just some run-of-the-mill asshole. This was highly personal.

But she persevered.

She trudged on for Maddy. For anyone else whose

mind he'd twisted. For herself. The stolen youths. And stolen lives.

His mind was a dark bottomless well where all good things got lost and corrupted. She could feel his hatred, anger, desire to corrupt. She could dwell on all the darkness and sin, could get lost in it forever in a heap of despair, but she had a job to do.

"Stop running!" The first command. He obeyed her. He had no choice. She was the puppet master now. Daphne surprised herself with how easily and naturally she took to controlling another human being.

If it were anyone else, she'd feel guilty.

"Show yourself." He was instantly visible to the cops and Miguel standing in the front yard of the suburban home.

"What the...?" Officer Price said in confusion and wonder. But Miguel wasn't all that surprised. He knew the guy had always been near. The man before them was muscular, in good shape for being middle-aged. His unmistakable tattoo, the snake wrapped around the eyeball, on display for all to see. The most surprising part of all to Miguel was that he seemed so…normal. A little intimidated even.

Miguel had seen murdering thugs. He'd seen gangsters with their pants hung so low they could barely walk. He'd seen criminal masterminds. This guy could pass for an everyday Joe. He wore jeans and a T-shirt that told of a concert from days gone by, his hair was slicked back and he had a neatly groomed goatee.

"Is this the guy?" Officer Price asked, not really sure what to do in this situation.

"This is him. Officer Derek Cayman is leading the task force. There'll be an arrest warrant for him soon," Miguel bluffed. He had no idea what they would find on the mountain, or who was going to lead the cold case, but he didn't want them to write this guy off. For Daphne's sake.

But Daphne held up a hand. "Just give me a minute with him. I've got this." Daphne sucked in a deep breath, steeling herself for the next thing she was about to undertake. She was going to have to go deep. And it was going to be disgusting.   But she wanted—*needed*—answers. How had they all gotten here?

First, Daphne forced Stryker to his knees. It was easy now that she knew how to do it. He couldn't resist, and this way she knew he wouldn't run. And then she went deeper into his memories, picking and digging for what she wanted to know.

She saw a little boy, cute, all-American, growing up in the Midwest. But he was different. He knew it. His family knew it. Everyone knew it. How could this kid just *know* things? They would call him freak. And that included his family.

He hadn't had the support of his family either, Daphne realized. *I wonder if Mark Kang knows how lucky and special his situation was?*

Stryker became an ostracized loner. And he'd hated it. He'd just gotten weirder and weirder, and more and more alone, as he'd gotten older.

When he was old enough, he'd escaped his home

state and hit the road for California. Because he could read people's innermost desires, it was easy enough for him to tell them what they wanted to hear. Unlike his childhood, in this new life with his fresh start he was well-liked, charismatic. Trusted.

He never told anyone of his "secret talents," and no one ever asked. Or judged him for it.

The popularity made him hungry for power in a weird way he'd never felt before. Growing up, he'd only longed for acceptance, but now that he was accepted, he wanted to level up. He didn't want just their admiration, he wanted *them*.

A twisted part of his psyche wanted to punish them for the pain of his bullied childhood. And he found that he could do it somewhat. He could get inside their minds and manipulate small things. A girl smiling at him. Being included in poker night with the guys. People feeling compelled to laugh at his unfunny jokes.

And it filled his depraved soul with a lust for more.

Daphne saw the day on Beck Winters' set when

Stryker first set eyes upon a young Daphne Winters, playing with her friend, Maddy. Looking through Stryker's eyes, she felt his instant pull to someone so like him.

Ostracized. Unique. A freak.

He didn't just want to get to know that little girl, he wanted to control her. He wanted to suck her psychic abilities out as if through a straw and make them part of his own being. Because he also sensed she was stronger than he was.

And he hated it, was jealous of it.

Daphne's stomach turned as she realized her Grandma Jean was right. This had always been about her. Stryker had been obsessed with a talent she didn't even know she possessed.

Only the plan backfired on him.

Not only was Daphne powerful, she was more powerful than Stryker and he couldn't control her once she caught on to his games.

Through Stryker's memories, she watched him approach Beck Winters one day on the set. The acclaimed film director had already come to like the charming stagehand, so when he mentioned that he knew Daphne was psychic and could help her get her abilities "under control," Beck Winters had been overjoyed at the prospect.

Beck and Alanna had always been worried about their daughter's awkwardness. They'd seen her quirkiness as a stain that needed to be rubbed out. Sure, you could have talents, just don't blurt them out everywhere the family went. Essentially, they were saying "stop embarrassing us."

And so Beck Winters had become a willing, yet ignorant, accomplice to Stryker's manipulations. Under the guise that he was "fixing" Daphne and Maddy, Stryker was able to get alone time with two eight-year-old girls. He toyed with their minds, used them for their abilities, and taught Daphne more than he bargained for.

At first, Daphne was a blank slate as much as Maddy. Stryker was able to control her, like when he forced her to play with the pickaxe and made her do his bidding. And Daphne had realized that something wasn't quite right, but the full extent of her capabilities to do to others what Stryker was doing to them didn't materialize until the fateful day when Daphne had gotten her face sliced open.

That's when everything changed.

His feelings of resentment and frustration toward Daphne had escalated. He struggled to control her, and when he tried, he found he was just teaching her new tricks. Abilities she excelled at. Maddy was talented, but she wasn't as powerful and natural in her abilities as Daphne was.

And he hated Daphne for it. And he wanted her dead. But he didn't want to have the blood on his own hands, when he had the power to make others do his bidding.

So, in the ugly little backwoods cabin one day, Stryker had "ordered" Maddy to kill Daphne. And so, robotically, Maddy had walked over to the table in the cabin and grabbed the pickaxe. Raising it high above her head, she stalked toward Daphne. Her eyes were glazed over. She wasn't in control of her own movements anymore. Daphne knew that Maddy would do it, and she wouldn't even be able to help herself.

Out of fear, Daphne used the ability that Stryker had been using on them. She reached into Maddy's mind, severed the connection Stryker had formed and forced her to drop the pickaxe. But she even went one step further.

She created a wall in Maddy's psyche that blocked Stryker from being able to control her ever again.

Stryker became irate, frustrated with his will not being executed as he imposed it. He lifted the pickaxe from the floor as Maddy cowered away from him, afraid of what he might do, but even more afraid of what *she* almost did.

Wanting to protect Maddy, Daphne stepped in front of him, blocking his path. But it didn't matter, Daphne or Maddy, he was angry at them both, angry at the world. Angry at his past, frustrated with his present. It all manifested into a complete rage.

But Daphne wasn't afraid of him. Even at eight years old, she understood him in a way not very many people could. But she wasn't going to just let him rage out on two innocent girls.

At the same time she grabbed his tattooed arm, she dug into his mind and forced him to drop the weapon.

As an adult, she realized her poor judgment at the time. But as a child, she was just reacting. Her face had paid the price.

Still in control of Stryker's mind, she forced him to drive her home first, then Maddy, where she whipped up the lie about playing with her father's tools. There was no way she was going to admit to her movie star mother that she'd been controlling people's minds. Again, as an adult she knew the logic was flawed, but kids only worry about their own repercussions.

If she had taken a moment to see where all this would lead, she might have been able to stop it.

"Get out of my head!" Stryker screamed from where he knelt on the grass in the San Fernando Valley.

Officer Price watched as he grabbed his head, shaking it violently as if that would physically force Daphne to loosen her psychic hold.

It didn't.

She dug in deeper as she yelled back, "I want my memories back, douchebag!"

Miguel encouraged the officers to stay back and allow Daphne to work. His heart was racing at the bizarre scene he was witnessing, but he knew undoubtedly that Daphne was in control. For a brief second, they locked eyes.

"It *was* all about me, Miguel." Daphne's eyes were heavy and sad with the weight of the past.

"We can make this right. Right now. You got this." Miguel nodded in encouragement.

Daphne steeled herself for the final stretch of digging in Stryker's reprehensible brain. She needed to know why he killed Maddy.

And it didn't take much work. She saw flashes of a little girl telling people on the set, including her father,

Xavier, what had really been going on with Stryker. And because of Daphne's block, he could no longer control Maddy.

She had become a wild card.

He wasn't afraid of law enforcement or imprisonment. Of course, he didn't want to be punished as a criminal, but that wasn't his fear. His fear was that he would lose the popularity he'd gained in Southern California. He was afraid his little world where he was likeable and not a freak would come crashing down all around him.

He killed Maddy to protect his reputation.

He found Daphne with her guard down, in the hospital where she recovered from her facial reconstruction surgery. She was sedated and unaware of what was about to happen. Removing the memories was harder than he thought—he had never been as naturally talented as Daphne. But Daphne not resisting him, he was able to finally get it done.

Beck Winters had been thankful that Stryker had

come to visit his daughter in the hospital. He'd still had no idea that he had willingly handed over two lambs for the slaughter.

And then Stryker attempted to rebuild the block he'd watched Daphne put in Maddy's brain. He wasn't fully confident he'd done it as well, but he'd take the chance. If he needed to, he could always take care of Daphne in another way later. He still hated her above all others.

But he had to silence Maddy. Right now.

She'd told enough people that he couldn't just ask for another "session" with her. That would be too obvious. So he kidnapped her and made it look like a random act of violence.

Making Xavier Laurens forget about everything Maddy had said was easy. And then he just had to lay low. But he'd stayed in the same old-fashioned cabin all this time. After a decade, he'd become cocky that his brainwashing and manipulation had worked—that he'd gotten away with murder.

But he'd underestimated Daphne yet again.

She swallowed the feelings of guilt—she'd need tons of therapy later—and focused on the task at hand. She forced Stryker to his feet. He tried to resist her, but all that came of it was him stumbling like a drunkard. She forced him over to Officer Price with heavy zombie legs, his arms outstretched before him in preparation for handcuffs.

"I want to confess." Stryker heard the words coming out of his mouth in horror. He couldn't stop them. He tried to fight Daphne but he was too weak. He always had been. Daphne knew that now, so the tables were forever turned. "I kidnapped and murdered Maddy Laurens," Stryker continued, "twenty-seven years ago."

17.

Without even fully knowing what was going on, Officer Price and his partner cuffed Stryker and put him in the back of the squad car. A confessed murderer was a confessed murderer and they had to at least process him.

Miguel ran to Daphne and hugged her with his good arm, lifting her off the ground as he did. His relief that this was all over was almost as overwhelming as her own. Even worse was the fact that he had no idea what was going on inside their minds.

"You did it. You finally got him!"

"I know the truth now, too," Daphne stated as Miguel lowered her gently back to the ground. "Maddy died because of me. I was the one to first create the psychic block—and I did it to protect Maddy, but it backfired." Daphne frowned at Miguel.

Miguel found a strand of blonde hair spiking off in its own direction. He smoothed it down, but it stubbornly kept bouncing back up. "You and Maddy were *both* victims. You ended up in the hospital and she died at *his* hand. You're not to blame for being powerful in your God-given talents."

Daphne snorted. "That's the line I always use on victims who blame themselves."

"It's true. He's the murderer here." Miguel pointed at Stryker in the back of the cop car. "Not you. You were just a little kid."

"My parents never knew the truth. Not even my dad. Stryker made him believe he was helping me." But there would be time to deal with that later. Two ghosts were watching the scene, and Daphne knew it was time to focus on helping them. She squeezed Miguel's hand. "But now... Gotta go to work."

"What have we been doing this whole time?"

"That was retribution. I was put on this earth to

help the dead, not the living."

Miguel didn't completely agree, but he let her have her space to do what she needed to do for Maddy and Grandma Jean.

Daphne walked across the lawn to where the ghost of a fashionable young lady and that of a cute little girl stood waiting to say good-bye. "I know Maddy's unfinished business, but are you good now, Grandma Jean? You ready to crossover, too?"

Grandma Jean laughed and the sound was melodic, warming Daphne's heart in a new way she'd never felt before. And Daphne realized she'd never taken these past few days to appreciate her grandmother. Sure, she was materialistic and superficial in life, but she was just a beautiful soul in her afterlife.

Grandma Jean laid a gentle hand on Daphne's arm. "I was here for you, honey. In a way I could never be when I was alive. I've been watching over you for years now. Keeping you out of trouble. Which is harder than it sounds, believe me."

"So you're my guardian angel?" Daphne scoffed.

"Just someone who loves you and didn't do enough to make it clear when she was alive." Grandma Jean tilted her head and her feathered, glamorous hair fanned out all around her. "But I don't really think you need me anymore, do you?"

Daphne could feel her grandmother's emotions, and they were powerful. There was a warmth encasing her chest that felt so comforting and whole. Daphne couldn't remember another time in her life when she'd felt so smothered in goodness. Perhaps Daphne's misguided family hadn't been the only ones to get it wrong. Perhaps she'd also been too quick to judge...and run.

"You're right, you know." Grandma Jean felt Daphne's emotions, just as she'd felt hers. "And there is still time. You can have it all if you believe in second chances. I know I do." Her smile was angelic and she literally glowed before Daphne, which Daphne knew was a sign that it was time to say good-bye. Her grandmother's ride to eternity was here.

"Bye, Grandma Jean." Daphne wanted to say so much more. She wanted to tell her thank you for watching over her all these years. She wanted to say she'd been wrong to judge her so harshly. She wanted to finally admit that she loved her grandmother. But the words didn't come. They wouldn't form in her mouth.

Luckily, Grandma Jean didn't need the words. "I love you too, little Daphne." And she leaned forward, kissing her granddaughter on the forehead.

Daphne watched as her grandmother's spirit softly faded into the glowing light. She'd watched many spirits cross over. Sometimes those spirits were family members too. But this one felt special somehow.

This time it felt like a tiny part of her soul was going with her grandmother. And Grandma Jean might have gone to the light, but Daphne could still feel the warmth. The love didn't go with her.

"Daphne." Maddy touched Daphne's arm.

She couldn't continue pining for her grandmother's soul. She had work to do. "It's time,

Maddy. After all these years, your soul can finally be at peace."

Maddy giggled the way only an eight-year-old can do, and suddenly Daphne was back on her father's film set playing with her young friend. Carefree playing and giggling, two good friends holding hands as they skipped. Nothing but the hope and promise of the future to surround them.

They had both been robbed of so much.

Maddy replied, "I've been at peace. I've been here for *you* all these years, too. I knew who my killer was and I knew you would catch him one day. But you were the only one who could stop him. And I knew you wouldn't rest until you did."

Daphne looked at her feet, more emotions taking her over. "I'm sorry, Maddy. I'm sorry for not protecting you." And she was. So much regret over putting Maddy in a situation that ended in her death. Wishing she had found a way to stop Stryker before he killed her friend. So much survivor's guilt over being the one who lived.

"Nonsense," Maddy answered, again sounding much older than she looked. "There's nothing to be sorry for. I've accepted my fate. It's time for you to accept yours."

"My fate?" Daphne tried to sense the clarity of Maddy's words, but as so often happened with Maddy Laurens, she was coming up blank. She was getting used to it, even if it was still annoying.

"Your gifts are stronger now." Maddy stepped into the ray of light that surrounded her, giving her the same halo effect Daphne's grandmother had had moments ago. "Continue using them to help people like us, who couldn't save themselves. But remember: help the living *and* the dead. You weren't put on this earth just to talk to dead people." Maddy winked and it made Daphne smile.

As Maddy started to fade into the light, Daphne whispered, "Bye, Maddy." Maddy waved back as she disappeared from Daphne's view, their spiritual tether undone.

Daphne was thinking about the meaning behind Maddy's words as Miguel approached her. Had she always helped the living as much as the dead? She supposed helping the dead was often also helping the living.

"Cayman called. I guess they have the body and the real murder weapon together where you told them to dig," Miguel explained. "That along with his confession should make this a pretty solid case. I've sent people away on less."

"Maddy's gone."

Miguel nodded. He'd suspected as much. "I'm not asking you to go back in there, but I find it highly unlikely this guy killed Maddy then stayed holed up in a cabin for nearly three decades. I'm sure there are other victims."

Daphne knew the truth in his words. She was *not* going back inside his degenerate mind, but she remembered flashes of other people he'd manipulated, injured, victimized. Getting him off the streets would help everyone. "I'll need to block his powers. Or else he'll just find a soft guard along the way and control them into opening the cell for him and letting him go. He's been using his talents for evil all these years, when he could have been doing so much good."

Miguel put his good arm around Daphne. "Well, they can't all be Daphne Winters, now can they?"

Daphne smirked but didn't respond. Had she defied the odds? Her parents and peers had mocked her just as Stryker's had him. She'd run away from it all just as he'd done. But somewhere along the way, she'd realized the power for change her gifts contained. Maybe deep down, guilt over Maddy *had* been a driving force, but she also had a chip on her shoulder to prove that her abilities were agents of hope and love.

She'd wanted to be everything her parents never were. She'd wanted to prove to herself and them that she was more than a façade. That she was real, and she could make a real difference in this world.

"I want to head back to Cayman, but there's someone I need to see first." Daphne twirled Cayman's keys in her hand.

"In Cayman's car? Look at the shape it's in." Miguel pointed at the crumpled front bumper.

"What?" Daphne shrugged. "It's still drivable." She opened the driver-side door and it resisted the effort. Everything was out of alignment. Over the hood of the damaged car she smiled at Miguel. "I sure hope he has good insurance."

18.

"Hi Dad." Daphne smiled at her father's awe-struck face.

Beck Winters had aged a bit, but nothing a little plastic surgery couldn't defy. He still looked a lot like she'd remembered him.

And Daphne had short blonde hair now and had filled out as she'd grown up, but otherwise she was still the little girl he remembered. He started to smile, and then remembered the strain between them. Putting his guard back up where he liked it, he crossed his arms and leaned against the front balcony of his Hollywood Hills home.

Like father, like daughter.

Daphne didn't fight it, she let the smile overtake her face. Miguel watched her carefully, loving the rare moments when she let her emotions show.

"It's okay." Daphne waved a hand in front of her face as if she could erase all the emotions with a swipe of her wrist. "You left me in the care of a murdering psychopath, and I blamed you for not knowing how to be a father to a psychic daughter. Let's just call it even."

"A psychopath, Daphne?" Beck Winters shook his head. "You always were so over the top."

"Only this time, it's accurate," Miguel chimed in. He'd never been a big movie buff or into celebrity gossip or anything, but he had to admit he was a tad excited to be standing on the property of the famous director. Even if they were just in his driveway and not completely sure they'd be welcomed in.

"Remember Stryker? He was a stagehand who said he could 'fix' me?" Daphne rolled her eyes. "Well, he murdered Maddy Laurens."

Beck's eyes went wide with the realization of how the daughter of one of his crewmen had died at the hand of someone else he trusted. "Do I need to ask how you know all this?"

"It's a long story. Let me just say he was playing us both. And it made me realize I blamed you for things I should never have blamed you for."

A moment of silence passed between them. This wasn't unusual for Daphne and her father. Neither were big talkers.

After a moment, Beck came around and descended the steep stairs that led to his front porch. "Who's this?" He nodded at Miguel.

What he didn't say was that he was sorry for being a terrible father. For not knowing how to be there for Daphne when she needed him. For not protecting her and her friend more carefully. But that he was glad she was here. And he was happy she was extending the olive branch.

Daphne felt all his sentiments come across, though. And it was enough.

Daphne slipped her hand into Miguel's. "This is Miguel. He's my soulmate."

Beck rolled his eyes. "Oh, sweet Jesus, Daphne. You and your new age mumbo jumbo." Daphne only smiled.

Miguel cleared his throat before saying, "Nice to meet you, Mr. Winters."

"Mr. Winters? Eww. Please don't say that. I am still hip and relevant." With his hair slicked back and his style en pointe even if it was casual, Miguel had to respect that he *was* still quite hip for a man his age.

Daphne rolled her eyes. "We already got the old-age-and-hollywood-don't-mix speech from Mom."

"You saw your mom?" Beck's eyebrow raised in such a way that made Miguel think maybe he was pining for Alanna as much as she seemed to be pining for Beck.

"Yeah, Dad. I did."

"How's she doing?"

"She's doing all right. Filming some cop show pilot."

Beck nodded. "Good for her. That's great. She was always so talented."

"Yeah. She always was," Daphne agreed.

An awkward silence passed between them all before Beck turned to Miguel. "And what do you do, soulmate?"

Miguel nervously cleared his throat again. "Homicide detective."

There was a beat while Beck processed this information. And then he tossed his head back and laughed. "Of course, you are."

Daphne tried to fight the smile creeping across her face. "It's not funny."

This only made her father laugh harder. "Yes, it is."

His laughter made Daphne laugh. And when Daphne stole a side-eyed glance at Miguel, she noticed he was stifling a laugh too.

When the laughter subsided, Beck sighed. "I knew you would never embrace the film industry. You were far too serious, even as a small child." He stared at his daughter very intensely. "Are you at least happy?"

"It would have been a complete waste of my abilities to make fluff with my life." Realizing she was again insulting her parents, and she was trying not to be that person anymore, she quickly pivoted. "What I mean is, you've helped people escape their problems and I help people heal from the loss of loved ones. With the occasional justice when we catch the bad guy." She shrugged. "So, yes, I'm happy with the life I've built."

In a rare show of affection, Daphne squeezed her father's hand. She hadn't talked to him, let alone touched him, in over a decade. She was surprised and pleased when he didn't pull away from her touch.

"And I need to say thank you, to you and mom. I was too stubborn at the time to realize that everything in my childhood led me to where I am today. And I like where I am today. I should never have blamed you. And I shouldn't have run."

There. She said it. It was out there now.

She looked up at her father and noticed he was cracking a soft smile. Without saying anything, he grabbed her and pulled her into a bear hug, kissing her forehead in the process. Still holding her tightly, he said, "I've missed you, kiddo. I even miss getting updates on dead people, believe it or not."

From her father's embrace, Daphne smiled at Miguel. Without words, she told him how much she'd missed her father too. And Miguel couldn't help but be happy for Daphne. She deserved to have a relationship with her parents, even if it was complicated, like most people's were.

To show his support, Miguel reached out and rubbed Daphne's back in small circles.

Beck noticed this and then reached an arm out and pulled Miguel into the bear hug. Miguel smiled at the moment, and also at the realization that a famous Hollywood director was hugging him.

And then Miguel's phone began to ring.

Beck let Daphne and Miguel go as Miguel checked the caller. "It's Cayman."

As Miguel answered the call, Daphne turned to her

father. "We're probably going to have to go."

"I know, saving dead people. But, Daphne." Beck squeezed his daughter's shoulder. "Don't be a stranger."

As Miguel hung up, he explained, "Actually, this time we're helping alive people. Officer Cayman wants us to go with him to talk to Maddy's family. Well, wants Daphne anyway."

"Duty calls!" Daphne saluted her father. "Bye, Dad."

"Bye, kiddo. I'm glad you came by."

"Me too."

Miguel opened the car door for Daphne, and she stole a final look back at her father before climbing in. She'd been running from him for so long. But he'd been running too. She knew that. She could feel it. Maybe they could stop running now and actually be there for one another.

"And, Daphne." Beck Winters put his hands on his hips. "I'd like to hear about some of your stories one day. They might make good movies."

Daphne rolled her eyes, but she smiled at her father. She wanted nothing do with his dumb movies, but she knew it was the only way he knew to connect. It was the Beck Winters language of love.

And it was a good start.

"Bye." Daphne climbed in the car as Beck lifted a hand to wave.

"See you soon, Mr. uh… Beck." Miguel corrected himself before joining Daphne in Cayman's car.

Daphne felt her father's emotions as they pulled out down the long, winding driveway. There was a sadness, but in a good way. He was sad she was leaving, and it warmed Daphne's heart.

Maybe Grandma Jean was right again. Maybe she just needed to believe in second chances. And for once in her life, she thought maybe she finally could.

19.

Derek and Winston Cayman were both out front of the ranch-style home in the San Fernando Valley. Derek was such a young carbon-copy of his father: big, broad-shouldered, gruff exterior. Daphne loved seeing them together on the job. It felt right somehow.

Miguel had barely parked the car, engine still running, when Daphne started climbing out.

Winston Cayman was beaming. "We got him." It was all he could say, but Daphne felt his elation, and mostly relief. And it matched her own. "Ya done good, Daphne. Real good."

"Yeah, we did." Daphne couldn't hold back, and she wrapped her arms around her old partner.

Derek Cayman didn't want to rush them along because he knew how long they'd been working on this case. He knew how much it meant to them. But he had a duty to the Laurens family. As Miguel walked up, he gestured toward the front door. "You guys ready?"

Daphne rolled her shoulders back. "For once, I actually am."

"We've been wanting to give this family an update for a long time," the older Cayman added.

Without any further discussion, Derek Cayman led the team to the front porch, rapping solidly on the front door. It had been a long day, and the shadows creeping across the entryway created the appropriate setting for the news they were about to give.

A pretty lady with soft eyes and a whisper of gray in her hair answered the door. "Can I help you?" But her expression told Daphne that she sensed why they were there. After all these years and all this waiting, detectives on her doorstep allowed her to hope for answers.

Derek flashed his badge. "L.A.P.D, ma'am. We have information for you on Madison Laurens."

Tears welled in her eyes. "Did you find her?"

Daphne waited for Derek to fill her in, but instead he moved out of the way, pushing Daphne and Winston to the front.

The older Cayman cleared his throat before saying, "Yes, ma'am. We believe we did. Pending a formal identification process. But her spirit led us to her remains. And to her killer."

Mrs. Laurens swallowed hard. "What?" Her voice was barely above a whisper. It was so much to process. Ghosts, bones, murder. All these years with nothing…and then everything all at once.

"Daphne is a psychic and she's been in contact with Maddy's spirit. Without Maddy and Daphne, this case might never have been solved."

Mrs. Laurens stepped forward and pulled Daphne into a warm embrace. For someone who wasn't used to hugging, Daphne felt like she'd gotten a lot of hugs recently.

When the woman pulled back, Daphne decided to come clean with the whole saga. No one could possibly understand how personal this all was to Daphne quite like the mother of another victim. "Maddy and I used to play together on the set of *Untold Angels*. My father is the director, Beck Winters. There was a stagehand on set that was drawn to me and Maddy because he was also psychic. Does the name Stryker mean anything to you?"

Mrs. Laurens shook her head. "No, but I never paid attention to all that stuff when Xavier told me about his work. If he mentioned him, I didn't pay attention."

"He was trying to practice mind control on us when we were both eight. Well, things got out of hand and as a result he wanted to silence us. He killed Maddy in the mountains. The whole crime scene down the street was staged." Daphne folded her arms across her chest. She was hesitant to say too much, since she knew it was her own deeds that had likely gotten Maddy killed. But she focused on what she always told victims: Stryker is the one who committed the murder. *He* was the reason Daphne's face had to be completely reconstructed.

If her parents hadn't been her parents, she might

have had a giant scar across her face her whole life that she didn't know the real story behind.

But Daphne could sense that Mrs. Laurens focused on the fact that Stryker had targeted both of them, and yet Daphne was standing here before her now. And Maddy wasn't. "You were able to escape?"

"Yes. I'm sorry." Daphne couldn't meet Maddy's mother's eyes. Suddenly she felt again like she'd failed Maddy, even though she was the reason Stryker would finally be behind bars.

Winston chimed in. "She took a pickaxe to the face. Don't let her fool you. She might not have died, but her life was forever changed."

Daphne looked up at Cayman. Good ole Cayman. He always gave her just what she needed. Pushed her when she needed pushing. Defended her when she needed someone in her corner.

Mrs. Laurens spoke directly to Daphne. "You should never be sorry. Why would I want another little girl dead like my baby? I'm *glad* you escaped. I know it sounds weird, but it gives me hope in a way." Mrs. Laurens was smiling even as tears threatened to fall. "Hope that even though my daughter didn't survive her attack by a monster, someone else did. Someone who could go on to be her voice when she didn't have one and continue until the bastard was put away." She reached out and squeezed Daphne's hand. "I'm thankful."

Daphne didn't know what to say in response, but she could sense the truth in what Mrs. Laurens was saying. She didn't resent Daphne for living when Maddy didn't.

And Daphne was thankful that Winston stepped in when words escaped her. "There'll be a long, painful trial ahead, but this guy's arrogance will prove to be his downfall. He thought because he was psychic, he could manipulate his way out of any wrongdoing. But he underestimated Daphne. He left a lot of evidence behind."

"And gave a full confession," Daphne added. Winston smiled at the news, giving Daphne a conspiratorial look. He knew she was behind it somehow.

"Will I...get her back?" Mrs. Laurens asked.

"Maddy? So I can bury her? We've been waiting a long time for the closure."

"Of course. Once the state is done with their investigation." Winston pointed behind himself at his son. "Officer Cayman will contact you for next steps."

Mrs. Laurens nodded and then looked at Daphne. "One thing I don't understand. I know you said he was attracted to your psychic ability. But what did he want with my Maddy?"

It hit Daphne so hard it was like a physical force. Maddy's family had had no idea she'd been a sensitive too. And why would they? Unlike Daphne, who couldn't keep her big mouth shut, Maddy had been able to harbor the secret. Even as a child she'd been aware of the importance of discretion.

"Mrs. Laurens." Daphne looked at Cayman but he just stared back, waiting for her to continue the story. "This may come as a shock to you, Mrs. Laurens, but Maddy was able to do what I do as well. She was a psychic medium too. It's partly how we'd become friends."

Daphne wasn't sure what reaction she'd expected, but it wasn't the huge smile that spread across the woman's face. Mrs. Laurens was happy to hear that news.

"Oh. She never said anything. How did you find out?" Mrs. Laurens asked so innocently, Daphne had to resist the eye roll that threatened to come.

"Let's just say it's definitely something psychics can sense." Daphne tried to force a smile back. She was finding that she did like Mrs. Laurens. Very much.

"It's simply fascinating. Are you...are you able to talk to her for me, even now?" Mrs. Laurens asked hesitantly.

Daphne nodded. "You don't really need me to talk for you. She can hear you. You just might struggle to hear back. But sometimes, if you keep an open mind, you just might be surprised how she communicates." Daphne paused and then added, "Is there something you want her to know?"

"Just..." Mrs. Laurens fiddled nervously with her hair. How many times had she talked to her missing daughter or her now-deceased husband in her mind because she'd go crazy if she didn't? This time just felt different because it wasn't hypothetical. "I just want to make sure she's okay."

Daphne smiled. She sensed Maddy hovering nearby. "Yes. She's totally fine. She wants you to know that she is with her father and they both watch over you and your family every day."

Mrs. Laurens started to cry again as she pulled Daphne into another embrace. She whispered into Daphne's ear, "Thank you."

"Lilacs," Daphne blurted. Maddy had forced it out of her mouth, so she felt the need to explain as she pulled out of the embrace with Maddy's mother. "Maddy said she's the one who always sends you lilacs. So when you see them randomly, you'll know it's her."

"Oh." The sound that escaped Mrs. Laurens's lips was almost a gasp. It was clear to Daphne that the message resonated with her.

"Do you have any other questions, Mrs. Laurens?"

Winston asked, bringing everything back to business in the way that Winston did so well.

"Uh, no. I don't think so."

"Derek, give her your card," Winston instructed his son.

Derek complied with his father's instruction. "If you have any further questions, ma'am, don't hesitate to reach out."

Mrs. Laurens hugged the card to her chest and nodded. "Thank you," she whispered softly. Sensing that was all there was to say, Daphne turned and started back toward Miguel. "And, Daphne," Mrs. Laurens called out, "don't be a stranger. I'd love to hear more stories about you and Maddy someday."

Daphne smiled back, and this time it wasn't plastered on. It was natural. "I'd like that. I'd really like that a lot."

More than catching Stryker. More than finally putting Maddy to rest. Mrs. Laurens forgave her. And it was making all the difference.

A tiny piece of her heart was finding that maybe, just maybe, she might finally be on the path to forgiving herself.

20.

"We've got our next case," Daphne told Cayman as she and Miguel stood on Cayman's front porch to say good-bye.

"Me too." Cayman smiled back.

"Derek took pity on ya, huh?"

"I prefer to think of it as appreciation of my skills and experience."

"Cold cases?"

Cayman shrugged. "Actually, any cases. I'll be acting as a consultant. I guess that's the modern way of saying they want my help but don't know exactly what to do with me."

"I think that's good. Better than falling in the river trying to catch a dumb fish." Daphne put her hands on her hips and smiled at her mentor. In so many ways, she owed everything to this man. She was just a lost kid with something to prove when she met him. He'd turned her into a psychic investigator. And she would always love him for that.

Cayman wagged a pudgy finger in her face. "Don't be knocking my fishing. I'll be doing plenty of that, too."

"You going to be alright?" Daphne asked. It somehow felt like she was abandoning him. How could he solve other cases without her? She felt like she needed his permission to leave for some reason.

Cayman sighed, sensing where this was headed. "I'll survive. Hell, I might even thrive. But you. You are the one that's going to be a superstar. I feel like I might have been holding you back."

Daphne smiled and then leaned in to hug him.

"Don't let this case make you soft, Daphne," Cayman said gruffly, but there was a twinkle in his eye.

Daphne pulled back, still smiling. She knew he only wanted what was best for her, like always. "You either, you big oaf."

Cayman thrust his chin out toward Miguel. "What's the new case?"

"I don't know a ton of details," Miguel started to explain. "My partner, Gina, called and told me there's a case that looks like suicide on the surface, but the family is strongly pushing toward a murder investigation."

"Sounds like you get all the fun ones," Cayman smirked.

Daphne scoffed. "I'll just ask the spirit what happened, and it will be open and shut."

"I admire your newly returned overconfidence, Daphne." Cayman raised an eyebrow at her.

"Daphne is also a consultant of sorts for the Fresno P.D.," Miguel explained. "So I am also hoping for this one to be an open and shut case." He raised his wounded arm, still in a sling. "I don't want to take any more bullets anytime soon."

"Maybe you should switch to cold cases." Cayman winked. Before anyone could respond to that, Cayman's beautiful wife, Helen, appeared in the doorway.

"Hello Daphne. Miguel." Helen Cayman smiled warmly. She was so gentle and tender, the complete yin to Cayman's yang. "Good to see you both again."

"Hi, Helen." Daphne raised a hand in greeting.

"Honey." Helen looked up at her husband. "I need you to take a look at the back deck. I think we have some wood rot or something."

Cayman put an arm around his wife. "Well, you two, duty calls."

"Take care, Cayman," Daphne said.

"You too, little one. You too."

"It was great to meet you," Miguel said, and he found that it wasn't just an expression. He truly meant it.

Cayman nodded in acknowledgement. "Go close those cases. And if you ever need someone to bounce ideas off of, you know I'm just a phone call away."

"Of course," Miguel responded. And he knew it was an honest invitation. He had a new friend, mentor and confidante in the retired, cranky cold case investigator. He didn't have the history that Daphne had with Cayman, but it was easy to see how she'd grown to respect and admire the man.

Cayman closed the door with a final goodbye and Daphne and Miguel turned back to Daphne's car.

Once they were inside the stuffy car, Daphne started the air conditioning immediately. She should be more used to the heat after living in Fresno for six months, but a true Southern Californian to the end, she only could handle about a ten-degree temperature span.

"Are we swinging by any parents before we leave?" Miguel asked.

Daphne looked at him and rolled her eyes. "I might finally have a bit more understanding of their perspectives, but I'm not quite ready to play family just yet. Trust me, they are both more worried about their own lives than mine."

"We're watching *Calamity* when we get home," Miguel stated, partially to goad her, but also meeting Beck Winters had reminded him of an old movie he'd enjoyed once upon a time.

"We're absolutely not. I don't watch Beck Winters movies," Daphne stated with no edge to her tone. It was a simple fact. He could watch her father's movies until his eyes popped out of his skull, but he wouldn't be doing it in her presence.

"What about your mom's movies?"

Daphne thought about it. Would she watch her mother's movies? Yeah, she might. She shrugged as she responded honestly, "I don't really watch movies."

"I don't really either," Miguel agreed. "So what do you do to unwind from ghosts and murders and suicides?"

Daphne turned onto the 118 freeway to begin the long drive back to Fresno. "If you're asking what I like to do in my free time, I guess I'd say going antiquing. Ya know, shopping for antiques? But I don't need to unwind from ghosts. It's just part of my life like eating is for you. You don't unwind from eating, do you?"

Miguel laughed. "You haven't been to my mother's house yet. You'll need to unwind from that meal, for sure." Miguel shifted to face her. "In fact, I'm taking you there when we get back. You are going to have a good old fashioned Mexican feast."

Daphne raised an eyebrow. "And meet your parents?"

"Yeah." Miguel smiled. "And meet my parents."

A flash of a short woman with her salt-n-pepper hair up in a bun flashed into Daphne's mind. "Okay. You met my insane parents and I already know I like your mom."

"What?" Miguel laughed even more. Sometimes it was hard to get used to her just knowing things. "My mom will love you. She'll think you're *'bien única'*. Quite unique."

"*Bien única*," Daphne repeated, the words feeling foreign and yet comforting on her tongue. She'd always wished she knew more Spanish than she did. "What did your father do for a living?"

"He was a contractor," Miguel answered. "Very handy man."

Daphne struggled to imagine a handy man and contractor raising someone so germiphobey as Miguel. In her mind, she saw a man covered in dirt and paint and not having a care in this world about it. "Was he a neat freak too?" Even though she already knew the answer.

Miguel laughed. "No. I'm a weirdo in my family. I mean, my mother does like things tidy, but she's never been compulsive about it."

Daphne smiled. "We're both weirdos in our families." The thought warmed her heart in a bizarre way.

But before she could probe further on the subject of Miguel's parents, an image flashed into her mind again. This time it was a mangled body on the side of the road. "Why does the family think it might be murder?"

The jolting change in subject was natural for Daphne, and Miguel knew her well enough by now to know this wasn't unusual, even if it did take him a moment to catch up.

Miguel shrugged, thinking about the case he was headed back to in Fresno. "Gina didn't give a ton of details over the phone. Mostly she complained about who she's working with while I am on leave."

Daphne thought about it for a moment and a name popped into her head. "Blue? Bell? Something with a B."

"Ball. Eddie Ball."

"Is he an ass?"

"Nah, it's not that so much. He's just got a very different style than Gina. You'll see." Miguel looked out the window as the San Fernando Valley whizzed by. "It sounds to me like the family probably just can't accept the truth about their son. It happens sometimes. Suicide can be very difficult to wrap your mind around."

"Well, I'll ask him when we get there, but I think the family might actually have good reason to question it, besides the emotional hurdle of suicide," Daphne stated as she changed lanes on the freeway.

"And you say that because...?" Miguel asked, truly curious.

Daphne chewed on her lip in thought. She didn't

have a fully formed intuition on this one yet, just something that wasn't quite sitting right with her. "I don't think he died where his body was found. Something about it is telling me that. And a dead man can't move his own body, so…"

"So there was at least one other person involved if his body was moved," Miguel finished her thought.

"So I'll ask the victim, but you'll need to find the person that moved his body. They just might be a murderer."

Daphne accelerated as they started the climb into the mountains that separated Southern California from the Central Valley. A psychic's work was never done.

She had another ghost who needed her. And she was on her way.

Join Daphne, Miguel and Gina as they work their next case in Book 3 of the Daphne Winters Psychic Investigation Series:

Dropped Dead